TRIAL BY FAE

DRAGON'S GIFT: THE DARK FAE

LINSEY HALL

For Uncle Jimmy.

1

MY BLADE SANK INTO THE DEMON'S CHEST LIKE A FORK through a perfect piece of cheesecake. Except grosser.

I crouched over his collapsed body and twisted the dagger, grinning into his sneering face. "And that's what you get for trying to eat children in my neighborhood."

The dagger tore up his heart as it moved. His mouth slackened and his eyes went dark. The big body beneath mine went totally limp. Dead.

Good.

I climbed off of him and left the blade in his chest. "You can keep that."

It was his, after all. The way I saw it, there was poetry in killing demons with their own blades. And I'd been a demon slayer for a while now, so I needed a challenge to keep things interesting.

The city street was silent as I made quick work of

checking his body for charms or weapons. Demons often carried valuable loot, and I wouldn't leave it behind. I patted down pockets and even flipped him over, wincing at the pain in my shoulder. He'd landed a good blow earlier, but it would heal by morning.

My hand landed on a small lump in his pocket, and I pulled out the little stone.

"Bingo." I shoved the transportation charm into my pocket and hopped up.

I put a hard butterscotch candy into my mouth and sucked. My sister called them my old-lady candies, but I didn't care. I'd quit smoking, and they kept me sane.

"You get him?" Aeri, my sister, called from the other side of the street.

I turned, spotting her stepping out from a shadowed alley, her white ghost suit speckled with blood. The ghost suit was just sturdy white tactical trousers and a top, but it had the ability to make her invisible. Totally badass.

Aeri's pale hair whipped in the wind, and her blue eyes met mine from across the street. This part of Magic's Bend was called Darklane—named for the dark magic practitioners who lived here. Aeri and I had made it our home ever since we'd escaped Grimrealm as kids.

I gestured to the demon at my feet with both hands and said wryly, "Ta-da. Dead and dusted. You get yours?"

"Nabbed the bastard at the end of the alley." She strode across the street to join me. "I got what info I could out of him. I think they were the only two stalking the city."

"Good. Nothing like a job well done." I'd report to the

Council of Demon Slayers that we'd finished the job they'd given us. I swung an arm around her shoulder. "Now I need a drink. The sun is coming up, and it's just about my bedtime."

A grin tugged at her mouth. "Let's do it. Fates know we earned it."

I gave the demon at my feet one last look. His body was already starting to disappear. If anyone else had killed him, he'd return to the underworld from which he'd come. Eventually he'd probably try to get back to earth.

But not this mean bastard. He was dead and gone forever, because I was a demon slayer, granted special powers by the Council.

Aeri and I walked toward our house, which was only a few blocks down from where we'd finally found the demons. The houses were quiet and dark as we passed, the Oliver Twistian street lamps flickering golden in the darkness. Most Darklaners were in bed, tucked behind the grimy facades of the ornate Victorian row houses that this neighborhood was famous for.

We reached our place, a grime-covered, once-purple Victorian structure that looked almost haunted. In our defense, we weren't slobs. Dark magic gave off a sooty substance over time, and it coated every building on the historic street, giving it a haunted Olde England feel. The buildings were all squished so close together that most of them shared walls. In the sun, you could see hints of the colors that the houses had once been, but that was rare.

It suited Aeri and me.

I led the way, climbing the short flight of stairs to the front door and disengaging the protection charms. I stepped into the elaborately decorated foyer of the main house. This was where we greeted visitors and did our Blood Sorcery business—a little side gig to the demon slaying—and the black velvet floral wallpaper suited the look. In reality, Aeri and I each had secret apartments on either side of the main house. Almost no one knew about them, not even our friends.

To say that we were secretive was an understatement, but we had good reason. We were Dragon Bloods—rare supernaturals who could make new magic. *Any* kind of new magic—stuff so powerful it could destroy the world. So rare that we were myths to most people.

The downside was that the government would happily toss us in the Prison for Magical Miscreants because we could be a threat. That was, if they didn't try to capture us and force us to use our powers for their own benefit. Turning us into weapons that could potentially destroy the world. Just like my aunt and uncle had tried to do before we'd escaped. Just like our childhood friend had tried to do when we were teenagers. My first real friend on the outside world, and she'd revealed our secrets to those who would hurt us.

Because of that, no one outside of our tiny, trusted circle knew what we were. No one could *ever* know.

I'd lived that life before, and I'd die before I'd go back.

"I've got time for a quick drink," Aeri said. "Then I've got to meet Declan."

I turned to her and waggled my eyebrows. "Big date?"

She grinned. "Yep. Brunch."

Last month, Aeri had met the love of her life, a fallen angel. I liked him a hell of a lot, and if I missed Aeri when she went on her dates, I sure as hell didn't say so. She deserved to be happy.

"Then come on. One quick one and you go get cleaned up for your date." I shuddered dramatically. "In the *morning*."

"Just because you're nocturnal doesn't mean we all are."

I laughed and led her toward my apartment, which hid behind a door that no one but she or I could see. Inside, each piece of furniture was a random antique and every bit of fabric a different color. Since I generally wore all black when out in the world, it was a nice change. There was a pile of knitting on the couch, which was one of my closest held secrets. It really didn't fit with my outside image, but everyone needed a hobby, right?

Aeri and I settled in the cluttered little kitchen, and I whipped up our drinks. I grilled her on her plans with Declan, enjoying our time together. For years, it'd just been me and her against the world. I was glad Declan was around, but I liked our sister time as much as ever.

By the time we'd finished our drinks—a Manhattan for me, a martini for her—I was ready to get my beauty sleep.

Aeri split for her place, and I headed into my bathroom, then stared into the mirror.

Fates, I look rough.

Though my eyes were tired and my skin pale, my black eye makeup was still impeccable, thanks to a special spell. It streaked around my eyes and over the bridge of my nose, sweeping back toward my temples like a mask.

A bit like Zorro, really.

And that was the point. It was meant to hide me.

Hide me from the past. From the family who had kept me and Aeri captive as children because of what we were. They'd forced us to use our Dragon Blood powers for their purposes. They'd try to do it again if they found us. Others would as well—we knew that from experience. We were the perfect weapons.

I shook away thoughts of the past and climbed into the shower. It was the one part of the apartment that I'd cared enough to modernize—all stone and chrome with a waterfall showerhead.

Ten minutes later, I climbed out of the shower, hearing Aeri shout goodbye and slam out of the house. How she had any desire to go places in the morning, I had no idea. I slipped into a robe and headed for the bedroom. I took my time putting away my fight wear and finally settled into bed. I fell asleep almost immediately.

For some fate-forsaken reason, the dream came almost immediately. On the bad nights, it always did.

I'd done everything in my power to forget the past. Aeri and

I had left it behind in Grimrealm when we'd escaped at fifteen. I wanted it to stay there.

But it would creep out in the night, when my defenses were down.

It started how the dreams always started...me, kneeling in the cold stone cell. Grimrealm was underground—right beneath Magic's Bend—so everything was cold and dark. All the time. But the cell was the worst.

The only light came from the window in the door, and most often, it was blocked by my aunt's leering face.

"Do it," she hissed. "Do it, or I will tell her what you really are."

"Please," I begged. I was only eleven, but boy, did I know how to beg. "Don't tell. Please don't tell."

I couldn't lose my sister.

"You're evil, little Dragon Blood. Your blood is black and dirty. Now spill it and make some magic."

Through teary eyes, I looked down at the dirty knife in my hand. My other hand lay on my knee, palm up, pale wrist exposed.

This was what my aunt wanted—if she even was my real aunt. My Dragon Blood gave me the ability to make magic. It was the rarest power in the world. The most valuable.

The more blood I spilled, the more powerful the new magic would be. If I lost enough blood—nearly all of it, nearly dying —I would create a new, permanent power. A magic that would change my own signature forever. Enough new magic, and it would become clear to the world what I really was. Every supernatural would be able to sense it. It might even make me as evil as my mother.

Then I'd have more to worry about than my aunt. More than the secret she held over my head like an ax. Every day of my life, she'd threatened me with it. The bogeyman in the dark.

"Do it, or your secret is no longer. Aeri will forsake you when she knows the truth about your dirty blood."

"No!"

I wasn't just a Dragon Blood like my sister. I was half something else...half something dark. Evil. I didn't have pure, pearly Dragon Blood like Aeri did. Like our father did. Mine had been polluted by my mother.

Aeri didn't realize what my oily, midnight blood meant, but I did.

It was proof that I was evil, like the mother I'd never met.

My aunt had made that clear, and worse, I could feel it inside me.

A darkness that threatened to rise up and take me.

It meant that I wasn't my sister's true sister. We'd never known our parents, and Aeri thought we shared both a mother and a father. We only shared a father.

My mother was an unknown species of evil supernatural with a magical signature of brimstone and putrid night lilies. It was all I knew about her. All I wanted to know.

I also knew that Aeri was the only thing I had in the world. The only person I loved. I couldn't lose her. Aunt had promised I would lose her if she knew.

Part of me didn't believe it. I was eleven, and I wasn't stupid.

Aunt would do anything to get me to make more magic. She would use me and use my fear.

But still...

What if she were right?

The proof of my evil was in my black blood, even if Aeri didn't realize it. She would when Aunt told her though. It was right there for anyone to see.

I dug the blade into my skin. Pain surged, and I liked it. I could focus on it, instead of my fears.

The blood welled, midnight black. It poured over my arm and onto the floor. I switched the blade to my newly weakened hand and clumsily carved into my other arm. More pain.

I smiled.

More blood.

It flowed to the stone around me, pooling warm at my knees. As it cooled, so did I.

"That's it," Aunt hissed.

I hated her. Hated her so much that I could have stabbed the dagger into her heart.

But she never gave me the chance.

These were the only chances she gave me—make magic, become a weapon, so I don't take the only thing you love.

As my body cooled and my heart slowed, I imagined the power that I would create.

Aunt wanted me to create a mind power that would allow me to control others—she, of course, wore an amulet to protect herself. Well, I'd create that power. But in a way to save Aeri and me. I would learn to appear in other people's minds...that's what I would do. Then I would send a message to someone on the surface to come save us.

I squeezed my eyes shut and focused on the vision. My head spun as my life seeped out onto the ground. I swayed where I sat, my breathing shallow and my skin cold.

Almost there. Almost there.

I had to almost die for this magic to become permanent, or otherwise it would just be temporary. Creating permanent magic was the only way that aunt would keep my secret. This wasn't the first time I'd done this, and it wouldn't be the last.

I fought unconsciousness as death threatened to take me. Once enough blood had flowed from my veins, I poured out my magic. I forced out every drop of power within my body, my head growing hazy. It mingled with the black blood, forming something new. Something different.

My stomach turned. Heaviness settled over me.

Then the magic changed. It glittered all around me, crackling with life and ferocity, then flowed back into my body. Strength surged through me, replacing the weakness.

My mind cleared, my breathing eased. My veins filled with blood and my body with magic.

New magic.

Permanent magic.

And my aunt laughed.

～

When a banging sounded at the front door, I jerked awake.

Heart thundering, I gasped, then tried to drive away the memory of the dream.

It was the worst of my past. I'd worked to forget—and I'd never told Aeri the truth about my lineage.

I'd meant to. Once I'd gotten out from Aunt's thumb and breathed the fresh air of the real world, I'd realized she wouldn't forsake me. I didn't doubt that now. Not as an adult. But I'd had fifteen years of brainwashing, and once we'd escaped, I hadn't wanted to think about it. Not talking about it meant not thinking about it.

Because I didn't want it to be true, even if I knew it was. Even if my midnight blood proved it was. Ignoring it meant I didn't have to face it. I didn't know who my real mother was anyway, and I controlled any genetic darkness inside me.

Blood didn't matter after all. Actions mattered.

And I was Aeri's true sister. We shared a father, and that was enough.

If the truth sometimes bothered me in the dark, I couldn't worry about it. If deep down I wanted to know the truth, I ignored it.

The pounding on the door continued. I groaned and turned to look at the clock. It was only ten a.m. "Who the hell visits Darklane at ten a.m.?"

No local ever would. Even those who lived in the rest of Magic's Bend and kept normal hours wouldn't dream of coming to a shop on this side of town at this ungodly time of day.

I covered my ears.

The banging continued.

Shit.

I squeezed my eyes shut and tried to ignore it, but whoever was out there *really* wanted to get in.

"Fine." I smacked my pillow and climbed to my feet, then pulled on my robe and stomped out of my apartment and into the main house. When I reached the front door, I peered through the peephole.

My eyes widened. "Holy fates."

2

THE GUY OUTSIDE WAS PROBABLY THE MOST BEAUTIFUL person I'd ever seen. And to be frank, I was blessed with a plethora of hot people in my life.

But this dude?

Otherworldly.

He had jet black hair like mine—only shinier, somehow, which was a real feat—and longish. It terminated around his shoulders in an artful disarray that was sexy as hell. Brilliant green eyes sparked with intelligence and coldness. His skin was pale and perfect, his granite jaw cut like a blade. The suit that he wore was nearly black, but when the sunlight hit it just right on the shoulder, I could tell it was the darkest green I'd ever seen. I knew good clothes, and damn if that thing hadn't cost more than most people's monthly mortgage. It fit him perfectly, tailored to fit his broad shoulders and spectacular height.

"I can hear you on the other side of the door." His voice was like smooth honey, and I shivered.

Then I scowled.

He had excellent hearing, that was for sure. What kind of supernatural was he?

I stepped back from the peephole and debated.

"I won't leave until you open up." The slightest hint of irritation sounded in his voice.

Jerk.

I turned toward the mirror that hung on the side wall of the foyer, inspecting my fresh-faced image and loose hair. The black silk robe that draped my form was fine for guests—but it was the lack of makeup that was *so* not okay.

I looked like myself.

No one except Aeri—and my old asshole family—had *ever* seen my real self.

I waved a hand over my face and called upon my magic, implementing a glamour that matched my usual look. Often I did it with makeup since the glamour could be a bit annoying to maintain, but in a pinch, this kind of magic helped me keep up my disguise.

Instantly, my reflection changed. The black mask of eye makeup concealed a third of my face, and my lips turned a brilliant scarlet. My hair rose up into a high bouffant that was *almost* comical but was definitely sexy.

As they said in Texas, 'the higher the hair, the closer to God.' I didn't believe in God and he certainly didn't believe in me, but that was beside the point.

For good measure, I did my clothes too. Earlier that

night, I'd been dressed in my black fight wear—tactical clothes that were practical and tough.

But this guy...

He must be here for some Blood Sorcery, and I had a very specific look for that.

My black silk robe turned into a midnight gown with long, tight sleeves and a slim silhouette that went all the way to my feet. The bodice plunged in such a deep V that most of my breasts were on display.

The last thing I added were shoes. Five-inch spikes that made me tower just over six feet.

I grinned, a catlike smile that was cold and just a bit cruel.

Perfect.

No one *really* looked at you when you were dressed like Elvira, Mistress of the Dark. They were too distracted by the makeup and the hair and the tits. I could walk right by my old family and they'd never recognize me as the frightened, abused girl I'd once been. Aeri had a disguise, too, but it was more sophisticated ice princess to my midnight whore.

I turned to the door and drew in a breath, then swung it open.

The man's eyes widened just briefly, flicking subtly from my face to my chest. But he had manners and a smoothness about him that made the gesture almost invisible. Even so, it felt like a caress. I swallowed hard and met his eyes.

There was silence for the briefest moment, and we did

what every supernatural does when meeting for the first time.

We sized each other up.

Every supernatural possessed a magical signature that corresponded to one of the five senses. Powerful beings had more than one signature. The strongest ones had all five.

Like me.

But I kept those on the down low, controlling them so others couldn't sense how powerful I really was.

This guy was doing the same.

I got a hint of the sound of wind whistling through trees and the taste of honey, but I could feel him protecting the rest of his magical signatures. I had a good sense for things like that—a natural gift—and he was hiding his power.

Probably a lot of it.

So what the hell *was* he?

My gaze flicked up to his face to find that he was still looking at me.

"We're closed," I said.

"Then why did you open the door?"

"To tell you to your face that I will gleefully eviscerate you if you don't stop knocking." I smiled sweetly.

"You do know the way to a man's heart."

"Oh?"

"Lead with force. I like it." His smile was cold, but honest.

I frowned. Most men quailed under my threats. Not this one, though. He almost seemed like he was flirting. In an icy way.

I narrowed my eyes at him. "What are you?"

"I'd like to be a client of yours. Mordaca?"

I inclined my head, acknowledging my full name. Only Aeri called me Mari. Mordaca was my public name, just like Aerdeca was hers.

I kept my gaze trained on his despite the faint discomfort of it. It felt like he could see into my soul, and I didn't like it. "Answer the question. I'm not letting you in here until I know what you are." The last thing I needed was a damn incubus in the house. "And tell me why you're here."

"I'm an elemental mage. Ice and fire."

"No, you're not. Your magic is too powerful."

He frowned, as if annoyed I'd figured him out.

"I can tell you're suppressing it." I tilted my head, studying him. He stood close enough that I had to bend my neck to look into his eyes. Even with my heels and impressive height, he was still bigger than me. He had to be a good six inches over six feet, with enough tightly coiled strength that he'd be good in a fight. Really good.

"And I can tell that you're suppressing yours."

"Takes one to know one, I suppose." I crossed my arms. We were at a stalemate. Two supernaturals hiding what they were and what they wanted.

Well, he was hiding what he wanted. I'd already told him I wanted him gone.

But now he'd piqued my curiosity.

I reached out and touched his shoulder, my movements quick as a snake's. My Dragon Blood gave me superior strength and speed. Combined with my natural ability to sense magic, I was able to get a feel for his true power.

I gasped.

The force of his magic bowled into me like a freight train. In a fraction of a second, I processed it all. His power sounded like wind roaring through trees and felt like the caress of the ocean. It smelled like an autumn day, crisp and fresh. The taste of honey exploded more powerfully on my tongue, along with the bite of something else. Something almost like a liqueur. He even had an aura—a deep green glow like the forest at midnight.

Before I could withdraw my hand, he surged forward and gripped my throat, pressing me against the wall. His touch was gentle but utterly immovable. My heart spiked into my throat.

He loomed over me, nearly blocking out the morning light from outside, his brow lowered. "You dare to touch?"

Yes, he was dangerous.

Fear, anger, and desire coiled within me.

I shoved them aside and drew a black obsidian dagger from the ether. The spell required to store weapons in the air was expensive, but worth it in scenarios like this.

I pressed the sharp blade to the base of his throat, making sure that the tip pierced the skin just slightly. Enough that a drop of blood welled. "Let me go."

He frowned briefly, as if surprised by me. Again, I was struck by his ethereal beauty. Intensely masculine, but otherworldly somehow. He was unique. Totally, completely unlike any man I'd ever met.

He was the kind of guy who wouldn't get a drop of blood on his impeccable suit as he slipped a blade between your ribs. But slip that blade, he would. I could recognize my own kind, after all.

It was impossible not to notice how close he was standing. Not a single inch of his body touched mine other than his hand, gently pressing against my throat. But I felt the heat of him burning through the two inches of empty space, straight into me. It was like an invisible wire connecting us, twisting tighter as the seconds ticked past.

He was dangerous. He was hot.

I'm an idiot.

The corner of his mouth kicked up in a smile. "Yes, I do think I like you."

Okay, not what I expected.

"Let me go." I pushed the blade a bit deeper.

Somehow, the tension between us only increased. The threat of danger, yes. But also attraction. My breathing grew shallow. I pushed the blade a little bit harder.

He let go of me and stepped back, straightening his immaculate suit coat. "My apologies. I'm not used to..." He searched for a word, and again, I wondered who the hell he was. "People."

"People? Everyone is used to people."

"Hmm."

"We'll just ignore that weirdness and move on, shall we? I need my beauty sleep, and it's getting late. What do you want?"

"I need a spell. Blood magic. My sources say that you and your sister are the best."

"We are, but we don't work for just anyone."

"I need an amplifying charm. The strongest one you can make."

I frowned. "Why?"

"My reasons are my own."

My mind raced. What kind of magic did he want to make stronger with an amplifying charm? They were difficult to create and required extremely rare ingredients. Therefore they were expensive. Very.

"You can't afford it," I said.

He smiled, all lethal elegance. "I'm sure we can come to an agreement."

"Fine. Two hundred thousand dollars."

"How about four hundred thousand and you make it right now?"

I resisted raising my brows, but it was difficult. Aeri and I did well in our Blood Sorcery business—this side gig was how we earned most of our money, since the demon slaying was more a labor of love than profit—but I'd named a hefty fee and he'd upped it.

I still didn't know what he was, but that was a *lot* of money.

"Cash?" I eyed his pockets. "I only take cash."

He reached into the pocket of his slim-cut trousers and withdrew a sparkling bracelet. Slender bands of silver twisted around huge, sparkling opals. They burned with fire from within.

I'd never seen anything quite like it.

He held it out, and I took it, stifling a gasp at the feel of the magic beneath my fingertips. These weren't just any opals—they were enchanted fire opals, forged in ancient flames of magic.

It was worth far more than four hundred grand. They were almost priceless.

Did he know that?

I looked up at him, catching the light of knowledge in his eyes.

Yes, he knew it.

And he was either too wealthy or too desperate to care.

And I was too avaricious.

Because I wanted these fire opals. I loved sparkly things. "Perhaps we can make this work. Won't you come in?"

"I'd be delighted."

As he stepped farther into the foyer, he seemed to fill the space with his sheer size. Now that I'd figured out his magic, he didn't bother to keep quite as tight a rein on it. It swirled around me, my senses lighting up with the sound of wind and the caress of water. It was nearly overwhelming to stand near him. Especially with the memory of our weird, violent, sexy embrace still in my mind.

I sucked in a careful breath. "Come this way."

As I turned to lead him to the workshop, I couldn't help but feel like this moment was going to change my life forever. And probably not in a good way.

I walked quickly to my workshop, feeling the weight of his gaze on my back. Normally, I might ask the name of my client. In this case, I hadn't even thought to. I'd been too distracted by his sheer presence. By how it impacted me.

We stepped into the long room at the back of the house that was filled with the ingredients of my trade. Shelves were crowded with jewel-colored vials of potion that glittered and gleamed. Dozens of bowls and knives and specialty tools were stacked in neat piles. Dried herbs hung from the ceiling, filling the room with scents of lavender and rosemary and sage, among other things that had no names but many uses.

A long wooden table sat in the middle of the space, with two chairs pressed against the wall opposite the enormous hearth. It was quiet and cold now, so I strode to the mantel and took a tiny pinch of magical powder out of the bowl that sat in the middle. I tossed it into the hearth. Flames burst to life, bathing me in warmth.

I could feel the man's gaze on me as I worked, and I schooled my features into passive interest as I turned. "Well, are you ready to get started?"

He stood by the door, his posture deceptively relaxed. I recognized that stance—it was the one warriors used when they were in unfamiliar places. Seemingly relaxed, but ready to fight.

"I presumed you would be the one starting?" he said.

"For the most part, but I'll need a drop of your blood for this to really work."

He frowned, clearly displeased.

"There's no way around it. This is Blood Sorcery, after all." I would use my own blood in the spell—it was immensely powerful—but I'd need his as well since he would be the one to wield the final charm.

"Fine, then." He took off his suit coat and draped it over one of the chairs. The dark gray shirt beneath looked to be just as expensive as the jacket, tailored to fit perfectly over his broad shoulders and taper to his narrow waist.

I moved toward the shelves to gather my ingredients. This was dark magic when practiced without consent, which was why I lived in Darklane. If I'd taken his blood without his permission, I'd be fully on the side of evil. But if you practiced it *with* consent and with good intentions, you were fine.

Try telling that to the government though.

Like many of those who lived in Darklane, I walked the

line between good and evil. Most were like me—not explicitly bad, but definitely iffy.

Aeri and I toed the line of legality these days, primarily because we worked for the Council of Demon Slayers. And because we weren't really interested in being assholes.

I gathered a bowl and two small silver knives, along with four vials of potion —red, green, blue, and yellow. I returned to the table as the man was rolling up the sleeve of his shirt, revealing a powerful forearm.

I laid the ingredients on the table. "What's your name?"

There was the briefest hesitation before he said, "Alexander."

"Hmm. You don't seem like an Alexander." I removed the stoppers from the vials and poured precise amounts of the potion into the bowl. The liquid sizzled and smoked upon contact, and I stirred it with one of the blades.

"Do you do this work often?" he asked.

"Are you trying to distract me from my question about your name?"

He frowned at me. "I'm just interested in your work."

"No, you're not." I pointed to his eyes. "You can't keep your eyes off this potion, and you just paid me an enormous sum for it. You need this. Badly. It's the only thing you're interested in."

He stepped closer, almost a prowl, until he stood so close I could smell the clean forest scent of him. Feel the faint heat of his skin. My heart pounded harder.

He met my eyes, then his gaze dropped subtly to my

breasts, which were spectacularly displayed by my dress. His voice lowered a bit, smooth honey. "I'd hardly say that's true."

I raised my brows. "Me? You're interested in me?"

"Who wouldn't be?"

"Well, that's true enough. I *am* amazing." Though the sexual tension between us had been real, this wasn't so much flirting as banter meant to distract. Flattery meant to drive me off my point. He was too smooth to stare pointedly at my breasts unless he wanted to throw me off. "But I'm not buying it."

"No?"

"No." I smiled at him, but it didn't reach my eyes. "I'm also not stupid. If you want to keep it a secret so badly, I'm not going to pry. This is just business."

He gave me an appraising look, seeming to like what he found.

"Now, will you please go get that silver knife?" I pointed to one that hung on the shelf.

As he turned to retrieve it, I quickly sliced my fingertip with the blade that I held. Pain flared, which I kind of enjoyed because I was weird, and a drop of black blood dripped into the bowl. The liquid sizzled and smoked. The wound in my finger began to close immediately.

The man returned with the knife and handed it to me.

"Thank you." I accepted the knife that I didn't really need. I'd just wanted to distract him from my black blood, which definitely wasn't standard. "Give me your wrist."

He held out his strong arm, holding it parallel with the

bowl. I gripped his forearm, my breathing growing short at the feeling of his muscles beneath my palm.

Energy zipped between us, an electric current that I'd never felt before. It lit up the magic inside me, making me shudder.

My gaze flashed to his.

His eyes were wide, his face pale. He felt it too.

"*Mograh.*" His voice rasped low, shocked.

"What?"

He blinked, eyes going sharp. "Nothing."

I frowned at him.

"Keep going," he said, expression stony.

I wanted to know what *Mograh* meant, but he clearly didn't want to say. I'd look it up later.

Carefully, I drew the blade across his wrist, making an inch-long slice in the flesh.

He didn't so much as flinch. I looked up, catching his gaze. Totally impassive.

"Do you not feel pain?"

"I do."

I couldn't tell it from his tone.

Blood welled, scarlet and bright, and I tilted his arm so it dripped into the potion. The droplets splashed onto the surface, and a hazy smoke rose upward. It smelled of the forest and the clouds. Quickly, it filled the room, swirling around us, making the air grow hazy.

The feeling of his wrist beneath my hand seemed to expand. As the smoke swirled around us and the spell worked, it became more difficult to see him through the haze.

I touched the side of the bowl with my free hand and fed my magic into the solution. It sparked and fizzed, magic swelling on the air.

The smoke filled my lungs as I breathed, making me lightheaded. I gripped the man's forearm, focusing on the tangible. But the smoke inside my head made my mind feel fuzzy.

This was so strange. It felt almost like I had a connection with him.

As if breathing in the smoke was like breathing in part of him. I felt like I *knew* him. Like I could be a part of him. That didn't normally happen when I made one of these charms.

The concern was driven from my mind as the smoke thickened in the air. All I could focus on was him. I could barely see him through the mist, but I caught glimpses of his flashing green eyes and his dark hair.

I didn't drop his arm, even though I didn't need to hold on to it for the spell. Because I just *couldn't.*

I was too trapped in this strange feeling. He was dangerous, that much was obvious. I could feel it, as if the smoke were whispering it to me.

He was the most dangerous man I'd ever met. He'd do terrible things to get what he wanted. He *had* done terrible things. Things he regretted.

He was torn up inside, some long ago torture residing in his soul like a sleeping dragon. But he was all lethal strength and determination, willing and able to move past it. To keep going.

It was that strength that drew me. That made my breath grow short in my throat.

The world seemed to close in on us. His scent filled my nose and the touch of his skin beneath my hand made me burn. The tension increased, drawing us together.

What was happening?

All I could do was feel him. Smell him.

I swayed closer to him. He moved toward me. We were two magnets, unable to fight it.

A low groan tore from his throat, one of resistance and longing.

His mouth collided with mine, his hands going around my waist. They were huge and strong, gripping me firmly as his hot lips parted mine. Desire fogged my head, and I wrapped my arms around his neck, falling into the kiss.

A sense of danger swirled around me, but I couldn't resist this. No matter how risky it was. The danger only fueled me. My tongue slipped into his mouth, and I pressed my body full against the hard, long length of his.

He cupped the back of my head, plundering my mouth. My mind swirled, my thoughts going blank as I acted on desire alone. The magic continued to swirl around us, the spell doing its work, but I hardly noticed.

The man's magic swelled on the air, increasing as we kissed. His touch grew rougher, less restrained. I surged against him, wanting more of it. More of him.

His mouth moved on mine, sure and skilled. I was

dizzy. When the prick of pain on my lip flared, I jolted and pulled back.

The mist had faded on the air, the spell complete.

I could see him fully now.

My jaw slackened.

He was the same insanely beautiful stranger, but he'd changed. *Shifted.*

His eyes had turned black, and silver horns had appeared against his head. They didn't jut upward like a demon's horns; rather, they appeared at his temples and ran backward along his skull, almost like a crown. Fangs had grown in his mouth, two long white points.

He was terrifying and sexy, all at once.

And I had no idea what he was.

He licked his fang as he stepped back from me, seeming almost startled that he'd shifted. Then true surprise entered his eyes. At the taste of my blood?

His dark eyes turned green once more, control returning. Interest flickered, and the corner of his mouth tipped up in a grin. His tongue touched his fang again, as if for another taste of my blood.

All the heat and desire that had filled me began to flow out, leaving me weak.

"You're a Dragon Blood." His words, so low and soft, made ice shoot through my veins.

No.

Somehow, the taste of my blood had told him what I was.

Quickly, I sliced my forefinger with my sharp thumbnail. Pain spiked and blood welled, and I reached up and swiped my bloody fingertip over his forehead. A swipe of black blood marred his pale skin, then disappeared.

"Forget of me, I will of thee." I repeated the chant twice, pushing my suggestive magic toward him. It was a small mind control trick that both Aeri and I had been quick to learn.

His eyes narrowed. "That doesn't work on me."

The earth felt like it had dropped out from beneath me. I reached for the dagger on the table beside me, instinct propelling me. *I can't let him leave here knowing what I am.*

His gaze moved from the dagger in my hand to the bowl beside me. Out of the corner of my eye, I could see the small golden charm that now lay within it. The spell was complete. The charm had formed from our magic.

Quickly, he reached for it and scooped it out of the bowl.

"I hardly think a fight would go well between us." He gave the dagger a pointed look. "And you may prove useful later, so I'd hate to hurt you."

Before I could fully process his words, he'd retrieved his jacket from the chair and slipped out the door. He'd moved so quickly that he'd looked like a blur through the air.

I lunged up from the table, sprinting across the room.

He wasn't in the hall.

Nor on the front step.

He was gone.

The bastard was gone, and *he knew what I was.*

I stumbled back into the house, my mind whirring.

Who the hell had that guy been? Where had he gone? I ran back toward my workshop, searching for any possible clues. Of course there were none. The only thing he'd left was the fire opal bracelet, which now lay on the table.

I picked it up and stared down at it, heart racing.

I'd use it to track him. It was the only way.

I gripped the bracelet tightly and closed my eyes, calling upon my seeker sense. A seeker was a type of Magica who could find things. I had only a bit of the power, though, and it didn't always work. No matter how hard I tried, it didn't work this time.

There was a block on the bracelet, a magic spell meant to prevent tracking like this.

Damn it.

I pressed my fingertip to the comms charm on my bracelet. "Aeri?"

My voice was hoarse with worry.

"Mari? What's wrong?"

"A man. He knows what I am." I had to tell her everything. This put her at risk, too, even though he had no idea that she was like me. But if I came under suspicion with the government, she would as well. We'd been joined at the hip our whole lives. Of course they'd suspect her.

"What do you mean, he knows? How?"

I spilled out the whole horrible story, even the kiss.

"Oh, Mari. That's bad." Her voice turned brisk. "But

don't worry. We'll track the bracelet back to him. Then we'll deal with it."

"Good. That was my plan. My seeker sense didn't work, so it can't be tracked that way."

"Declan has some equipment that may help if the Fire-Souls can't."

The FireSouls were our friends who could track anything of value, though I had a feeling that the protection charm on the bracelet would prevent even their impressive powers from working. I'd try anyway.

"Declan had to go to angel headquarters—something about a stolen bomb that's super deadly—so I'll come over now. When he's back, he can help."

"Thank you. I'm headed to the FireSouls' place to see if they can help."

"Good luck. I'll be home soon, and we can go together."

I cut the connection on the comms charm and hurried to the bookshelf in our workshop. It took several books, but I finally found the meaning of *Mograh*.

I stared at it, dumbfounded.

It meant *my love* in the Seelie Fae language, which was similar to Scots Gaelic. But the true meaning was *fated mate*.

Somehow, I was the one woman made for him.

That's why he'd looked so shocked. And maybe even why I'd had that insight into who he was when I'd been performing the spell.

But he'd ignored it. He didn't want it.

Which was fine by me. Perfect even. Because no way I

was signing up to be some mysterious man's fated mate. I had other things to be doing.

I snapped the book closed and went to my apartment, my mind racing. Despite the glamour, I was still wearing a bathrobe and would need to change before heading to the other side of town.

Quickly, I painted the black mask over my eyes and did my hair up in a high bouffant ponytail. I found a fresh set of black fighting leathers and put them on, then grabbed my boots. I shoved the enchanted bracelet into my pocket.

Within minutes, I was heading back into the foyer of the main house. Aeri and I never departed out of our secret apartments, which were hidden in buildings on either side of the main house. No one knew we actually owned them, and since their front doors were never used, the neighborhood thought they were abandoned.

As soon as I'd stepped into the main foyer, a shrieking alarm went off. Red magic rolled over the ceiling, sparking and bright.

My heart jumped into my throat.

Shit shit shit.

Red alert. A freaking red alert.

4

THE ALARM BLARED, SHRILL AND HORRIBLE.

The Council of Demon Slayers was calling.

Under no circumstances could I ignore it. We *owed* the Council. They'd helped smuggle us out of Grimrealm years ago when we'd escaped. And whatever they needed us for was serious. Only the worst demons got a red alert.

The front door slammed open, and Aeri ran in, her eyes wide. "Red alert."

"Let's go." I turned on my heel and headed back toward our workshop.

Together, we approached the huge rectangular table in the middle of the room. The fire had died down, but I could see by the light of the hallway. I stopped at the corner of the big table and pressed my hand to the wood. Aeri did the same, and magic sparked on the air. The table levitated and drifted to the side of the room.

Together, we approached the hidden trapdoor in the

middle of the floor, which was normally hidden under the table and completely invisible. I sliced my fingertip with my thumbnail and let a drop of blood fall to the ground. Aeri did the same. When my black blood joined her white blood on the stone, magic filled the air.

The door disappeared. Narrow stone stairs led deep into the earth, and I raced down them. It grew colder and damper as I descended. The wound on my finger was already healing, courtesy of an enchantment. It only worked on my finger, but it came in handy when you had to use blood magic so often.

About halfway down, metal spikes shot out of the wall. I stopped abruptly. The points pressed into my skin, not breaking the surface but threatening all the same. This place was so important that we'd installed safety measures to protect it.

Recently, we'd changed them to the metal spikes, and I still wasn't used to them.

My heart thundered as I carefully shifted my hand and allowed one of the spikes to pierce my skin. The thirsty metal drank up my blood, testing me. Eventually, the metal spikes retracted back into the wall, allowing me to pass. Aeri would go through the same test, but I didn't look back to check on her. She'd be fine.

I sprinted down to the next level. The steps lengthened here, forming a small platform. I stopped, standing perfectly still. Quickly, pale gray smoke began to fill the air. I breathed it in, trying to ignore the memory of the smoke that had entranced me into kissing the mysterious man.

I mean no harm. Let me pass. I recited the thought in my mind, letting the smoke fill my lungs. It froze my limbs solid, making it impossible for me to move. The enchanted fog would read my true intentions and make sure they were pure.

If they weren't, I'd stand here frozen forever.

Over and over again, I repeated the mantra. Eventually, the smoke faded and the freezing grip on my muscles ceased.

I hurried down, finally reaching the cavern far below the main house. It'd been no coincidence that we'd chosen this place to live. Every demon slayer had a well of power near their home. It was our conduit for contacting the Council, and the magic in the pool could be used to enhance our own power.

Very rarely, we'd bring people down here to perform important magic—but only people we trusted. Even then, we didn't tell them what the pool really was. Instead, we told them that we'd bought the place and the pool from a witch who retired to Florida to play Canasta.

They always bought it.

We were excellent liars.

The pool sparkled in the middle of the dark cavern. Aeri joined me, and we approached. I yanked off my boots and socks and stepped into the cool blue water. Aeri followed, and we gripped hands.

"Here we be, let us see," we chanted, our voices growing louder.

Tension thrummed in my muscles as we waited.

Enchanted water lapped at my legs as I chanted, "Here we be, let us see."

Magic swirled on the air, glittering blue and bright. It moved faster, a tornado of sparkles that was almost blinding. The air popped. The magic faded.

A figure rose from the middle of the pool. Her form was ephemeral, her features strange. She was more ghost than person, though not quite either. Often, she was crotchety and irritable, but I'd grown to care for her.

"Agatha." I inclined my head out of respect.

She was our contact with the Council, an unusual type of supernatural who could travel through Wells of Power. She drifted toward us, her mouth set in a firm line.

"What is it?" Aeri asked. "What's gone wrong?"

"Hold your horses." She stopped in front of us. "We have need of you. There is a dark power rising in the Fae Kingdom of the Seelie Court."

"The Seelie Court? In Scotland?"

Holy fates. Like the man I'd just met. I thought I'd never seen a Seelie Fae, but I'd been wrong. They were so reclusive and mysterious that they'd achieved almost mythical status amongst supernaturals. Considering that our numbers were made up of vampires, witches, mages, and shifters, that was saying something. Other Fae walked the earth and weren't uncommon, but the Seelie Fae were never seen.

Except I'd just seen one.

And I might be his mate.

Which was something I needed to take care of, since I definitely didn't want to be.

"The very same," Agatha said. "There is demonic energy coming from their kingdom in greater quantities than we've ever seen. It has a signature of brimstone and putrid night lilies, but it is impossible to trace as it is completely unique."

My heart stuttered.

Brimstone and putrid night lilies.

Holy fates. My mother.

According to Aunt, that was my mother's signature. And like Agatha had said, it was completely unique. Could it possibly be her?

"How did demons get there?" I asked, trying to play it cool. Agatha didn't know about my mother. Only I did.

"We don't know. Perhaps the same way they got here—a Fae helped them escape the underworld. But whatever the case, the power is growing greater. More than a hundred Fae have been mysteriously killed."

A hundred? Holy fates. "And they've asked for our help?"

"No."

"No?" I frowned. "So they're handling it themselves?" I had no idea what kind of defenses they had there. *Could* they handle it?

"They aren't even acknowledging that it exists. We sent an emissary to meet with the king. He denied it right to our faces. We could feel the energy, but he said we were mistaken."

"He was lying," I said. Some Fae couldn't lie, but not all.

"We think he was."

"Then he's the problem," Aeri said.

Perhaps he was in league with my mother? Who was possibly some kind of demon?

"Most likely, yes. If the energy continues to grow—which we believe it will—it could destroy their entire kingdom. Their entire realm. Once it has done that, it could spread from there to earth and throughout the world."

Oh, shit. The rest of the world? "Where is the energy coming from? Multiple demons invading? Or just one very powerful one?"

"We don't know. That's a possibility. Or a demonic spell."

"So we have no idea," Aeri said. "Just that it's growing and people are dying. Are the people there concerned?"

"They can't sense it," Agatha said. "Not the way that we can. They aren't familiar with that type of magic and don't easily recognize it. Whereas we are experts, keeping track all over the world."

"What about the deaths, though? Surely they notice those."

"They're anxious. They don't understand the cause, from what we've been able to determine. But we can't get past the king to speak to them."

He was a problem, definitely.

"Which raises a question," Aeri said. "Why us? Normally we work Magic's Bend."

All demon slayers had a particular turf that they protected. When we'd escaped Grimrealm, which was located directly under Magic's Bend, we'd wanted to go as far away as possible.

The Council had put us here, instead. Hence my disguise, which had become just as much a part of me as my DNA by this point.

"You're perfect for the job, Mordaca, with your seeker sense and powerful ability to sense magical signatures. And you look a bit like the fae, which will allow you to blend in. They will hopefully trust you more easily, which will be helpful if you are spying on their king."

Yes. I had to try. If my mother was involved with this, I had to. And perhaps I could even find the Seelie Fae and shut him up about what I was. And also break this fated mate bond. "I'll do it, of course. But how do I get in? The Seelie Fae are notoriously secretive."

"And that is where we have gotten a little bit lucky," Agatha said. "This year—this week, in fact—the Seelie Fae are hosting their annual tournament. Trials open to any supernatural who wants to test their magical mettle against the rest of the world, with a fabulous prize at the end."

"And you want me to enter."

"It will get you into their realm. Get you close to the king, as he will be the main judge."

It was genius. I looked at Aeri.

She nodded. "You'd do well in the trials. I can track the origin of your bracelet while you're gone."

"Thank you." I'd tell her later that it might not be necessary if I could find him in his realm. I looked at Agatha. "I'll do it."

After Agatha left, I had only hours to prepare. She'd given me directions to the entrance of the Seelie Fae Kingdom, along with an amulet that was my invitation. I was meant to use it to get in and present it to the Fae guardian at the border.

As quickly as I could, I packed a bag full of potentially valuable potions and stashed it in the ether. I could draw it when needed. I then removed all iron weapons from the ether, leaving only the copper. Iron was strictly forbidden in the Fae realms as they were allergic to it.

Actually...

For good measure, I stuck one iron dagger back in the ether. I didn't have to take it all the way there, after all. Maybe I could find a place to stash it just outside their realm in case I needed it.

Once I was ready, Aeri hugged me. She gripped the fire opal bracelet. "I'll find the guy who gave this to you."

"Thanks." I stepped back. "I'm off now. Call me with any updates."

"Be safe."

I saluted, then called upon my transportation magic, imagining my destination. The ether sucked me in and whirled me through space, making my stomach turn and my breath grow short.

It spat me out on the green grass in Kilmartin, Scotland, a region renowned for its ancient heritage sites. Hundreds of stone circles, petroglyphs, chambered cairns, and hill forts littered the area. It positively reeked of Fae magic, though the Seelie Kingdom was located in another realm that existed parallel to this one.

They were technically the good Fae in this region, while the Unseelie Fae were the bad Fae.

Nothing was ever that simple though.

I spun in a circle, breathing in the cool, windy air as I inspected the mountains surrounding me. They soared in the distance, surrounding the flat green plain on which I stood. The sun dipped toward the horizon as twilight arrived.

It was the perfect time to try to gain access to the Seelie Kingdom. The Fae were a twilight people, existing at the borders of day and night, this realm and the other, the past and the present.

The magic in the air was different than any I'd ever felt. Ancient and heavy, with a hint of the whimsical. Behind me, I found a long row of standing stones. They were flat and thin, spearing toward the darkening sky with a majesty suited to their age.

The stones themselves were thousands of years old, laid down by the ancient Fae to mark the entrance to their world. Humans thought that their own ancestors had created the huge monuments, though they'd never been able to figure out exactly why.

They were wrong.

These were Fae stones, though humans had taken to worshiping them almost as soon as the Fae had put them up.

I approached one and reverently rested my hand against the flat, rough surface. Magic flowed into me, almost familiar.

Where had I felt that before?

It was unsettling, but I couldn't quite place it. My gaze was drawn to round indentations in the stone that looked intentionally placed, but I had no idea what they were for. I ran my fingertips over them, studying each one in turn.

The sun dipped deeper in the sky. Twilight was nearly gone.

I needed to find the entrance before it was too late.

I made my way down the row of stones, headed for the end. The magic seemed stronger there, the air almost sparkling with it. When I reached the final stone, it was clear that I stood at the entrance to the Fae realm.

I could *feel* it. There was a door. An invisible one, but a door all the same. My soul ignited at the feel of it. It was just like standing at the edge of a cliff, waiting for the fall.

Before I could enter, I needed to hide my iron blade. I took it from the ether and jogged to a copse of trees about twenty yards away. It would be a pain in the ass to retrieve in the future, but I was obsessed with being prepared.

I buried it shallowly in the dirt, then returned to the

invisible door. I stepped forward, moving toward the strongest magic. I managed two steps before I slammed into an invisible barrier.

Blocked.

Agatha hadn't mentioned anything about this. She must not have known.

I studied the standing stone closest to me.

There was a faint glow in the middle of it. One of the small round indentions was lit up with a host of sparkling fairy lights.

I tilted my head and pursed my lips. "Hang on a sec."

I pulled the medallion from my pocket. Agatha had told me to present it to the first Fae I met, and perhaps I would. But I wanted to try something first.

Slowly, I approached the stone. It towered above me, twice as tall and three times as wide as I was. Thin patches of green lichen covered the surface, but it was the glowing indentation that I was interested in. Someone had carved that little circle into this rock at some point, long ago. It'd taken ages no doubt, so it had to be for a purpose.

I lined up the medallion with the circular indent and pressed it inside. Magic sparked, bringing with it the sound of birdsong and the last warm rays of the sun. To my left, where the portal magic had been the strongest, the air vibrated.

I turned to look. A door was appearing. It was made of twisted, pale tree limbs that were so artistically interwoven that I gasped. Around the door was an arch created of the same limbs, but the tops bloomed with bright white flowers.

Breath held, I withdrew the medallion and clutched it tight, then stepped toward the door. As I approached, it swung open.

Magic bellowed out, a dozen different signatures tumbling over each other. They were all earth-based—the sound of tree limbs rustling, the scent of a calm lake, the feel of grass beneath my feet, and wind in my hair.

"Here goes nothing," I muttered as I stepped through.

I'd been in a lot of amazing places in my life, but it was *rare* that I got to go to other realms.

The Seelie Fae Kingdom?

Hell, that was the rarest of all. A place so secretive that I had been halfway sure it didn't even exist.

But it did.

I stepped out into a forest grove. It was twilight there as well. The sun had just dipped behind the enormous trees and shed a pink light across the entire sky. It was edged with dark gray as night fell swiftly.

I craned my head back to inspect the trees. Wonder filled me at their size. Each one was at least four hundred feet tall. Even bigger than the redwoods, with silver gray trunks and deep green leaves.

Except there was a darkness here, just like Agatha had said. I could feel it in the air, faint but true. Dark magic like a slick of lake slime against your skin. And it smelled vaguely of brimstone and putrid night lilies.

I shivered, my heartbeat jumping.

"Welcome." The voice floated on the air from behind me.

I whirled around, suppressing my usual fighting instinct.

She'd said *welcome* after all.

The woman who stared at me looked more Fae than anyone I'd ever seen. Her skin was milk pale and her hair an icy blonde. Bright lavender eyes assessed me, and her pointed ears twitched.

Did she sense the darkness as well?

She didn't seem to.

Behind her, an enormous city rose in the distance. It looked nothing like the cities on earth. Half the buildings were built into trees, and the others were so ornate that they looked like decorative cakes. Fairy lights floated in the air—slightly bigger than fireflies and pale white.

"I am here for the competition." I held out my medallion, and she took it.

Carefully, she inspected it, then slipped it in her pocket. "Do you bring iron with you?"

"No."

"I'll check all the same. You have quite an arsenal stored in the ether."

"You can feel that?"

"I guard the Fae realm. Of course. It's my job."

"Okay." Quickly, I began to pull all my weapons from the ether. They appeared in my hand at my command, and I laid them on the ground. Daggers, sword, bow and arrow. My pouch of potions.

The Fae knelt and hovered her hand over each one. Finally, she stood and nodded, satisfied. "You may continue on. I will call a carriage for you."

She whistled and waved her hand while I knelt and repacked my weapons. When I stood, I spotted a fabulous open-air carriage rolling up the lane. It was made of the same pale, twisted wood as the door had been, with highlights of sparkling silver. The two steeds that pulled it were silver-winged stags, their horns shooting up toward the sky.

The carriage pulled up alongside, and the driver peered down. He was tall and strong, with jet black hair and green eyes. Just briefly, he reminded me of the man I'd seen in my shop earlier that day, but the feeling faded quickly.

Next to him sat a tiny figure with wrinkled skin and huge eyes. The creature—a male, I guessed—wore a blue tunic that looked almost medieval, and had unnaturally long fingers. I didn't want to stare too long, but I did want to figure out what he was. A hobgoblin or brownie, perhaps.

"Ready to go?" the Fae man asked.

"Ready." I climbed into the carriage.

He flicked the reins, and the stags took off, trotting down the lane. The massive trees rolled by on either side.

The small, wizened figure hopped up on its seat and turned around to peer at me. "You here for the games?"

"I intend to win."

"You'll probably die."

"I won't."

He shrugged. "Lots do. But the prize is worth it. Any wish you want. Granted."

"Any wish? Really?"

He nodded.

Wow.

The wizened creature looked at me with squinted eyes, then gestured to his face. "What's with all the black around your eyes? Your soul seeping out or something?"

"Eh, not quite?"

The figure grunted. "Well, try not to die too quick. I like you."

Yikes. "Thanks?"

He turned around and flopped back into his seat. The city rolled ever closer, with the main castle soaring above the houses. The famous Fae Court. Ornate towers connected by arched walkways soared through the air.

We passed through the city streets, rolling by dozens of Fae going about their daily business. And it seemed they really couldn't feel it. They were different than the ones I'd seen walking the streets of Magic's Bend.

For one, they didn't all have wings. At least not visible. Maybe they didn't even have them. But the biggest difference was their power. These ones seemed much stronger. As if the earth-walking Faes' magic had been diminished by being away from the Fae realms.

The closer we got to the castle, the stronger the dark energy in the air.

Demonic, definitely.

Many of the houses had black cloths draped over their doors. They were very different than the otherwise pale fabrics that hung in the windows.

I pointed to them. "What's with all the black?"

The hobgoblin—or brownie, I didn't know how to ask—frowned, his eyes turning sad. "The deaths. They came two months ago. Took over ten percent of our people."

Fates, that was so many. Horror sliced me. "How?"

"We don't know. They disappeared. Later, their hearts were found, shriveled and rotten."

Oh, shit. And the king didn't want our help? "But the deaths stopped two months ago?"

"Just about, yes. Maybe longer."

"Why?" Agatha hadn't mentioned that. Maybe she hadn't known. It was difficult to get information from here.

"We have no idea. We are waiting for them to start again."

I shivered and sat back in my seat, watching the town carefully as we passed, searching for any clues to the dark magic that grew stronger as we neared the castle. Still, no one seemed to notice it. I was particularly skilled with sensing it, but I'd have expected some of them to be able to smell it or feel it. The signature was distinct. Decay and mold. Rot and filth. In this case, brimstone and putrid night lilies.

Extremely out of place in this otherwise beautiful wonderland.

The castle loomed above as we approached. "The king

must be a pretty powerful guy if he lives in a place like this."

The wizened little figure hopped up and turned back around, a big grin revealing a mouthful of fangs. "Oh, he is." He shuddered. "Mean bloke, though. Keeps to himself since he took the throne."

Apparently he liked to gossip, and that was good for me. "When was that?"

"In the spring."

"So just a few months ago?"

"Yes. Just about."

Hmm... How did that timing work with the deaths? "Two months or three? Four?"

"Two."

Interesting. "How is he mean?"

"Always scowling. Silent. Hardly merry like a Seelie Fae should be. Almost no one ever sees him, in fact. The Court is in session less than it ever has been. He's not keen on others. And he says he's trying to solve the murders, but we don't believe him."

"Interesting. Any idea why?"

"Mean bloke?"

That wasn't exactly a great answer, or a confident one, but it'd have to do. Never insult your source. Rule number one of trying to sweet-talk info out of people. They might clam right up if you insulted them.

I nodded. "I know just the type."

"The worst, aren't they?"

"Definitely."

The little figure shrugged. "Most of us are afraid of him. He's ruthless. Some say cruel. Only his inner Court ever sees him, and that's rare."

"*Is* he cruel?"

"Hard to say. Never seen any indication he isn't. He's got some horrible things in his past, though."

I leaned forward slightly. This was good shit. "Like what?"

The little figure clammed up, his mouth flattening into a line. "Shouldn't say no more."

Damn it. I needed to keep him talking. Get him comfortable enough to spill the details later. "But he's hosting the games? Why?"

"It's been years since we've had one. Maybe for his own entertainment?"

"Sounds like a peach of a guy." I tilted my head back to inspect the underside of the castle wall as we passed through a gate. The stone was a pale silvery gray, shot through with minute sparkles of mica. I looked back at the tiny troll, ready to ask more questions.

But the carriage rolled to a stop at the side of the castle.

"We're here." The driver turned around to look at me, then gestured to the ground. "Your stop."

"Thanks for the ride." I climbed down and approached the arched entrance at the base of the castle. Above, dozens of windows gleamed in the light. Trees grew right inside the castle walls, their branches weaving through the stone. It should be impossible, but not here.

"You're not in Kansas anymore," I muttered as I

approached the two guards who stood on either side of the archway.

They were dressed in gray-blue tunics and trousers, the fabric woven with threads of silver. Their hair was drawn back to show off their pointed ears, and they carried tall wooden pikes tipped with silver.

The guards' eyes flicked to the carriage, then they nodded. The one on the left spoke in a gravelly voice. "Come with me. You will join the other competitors."

He led me into the depths of the castle. It should've been dark and dank and gross down here, like in most castles.

But not in a Fae castle. The passageway was wide, with a high arched ceiling and smooth stone floor. Torches dotted the walls every ten feet, each filled with sparkling fairy lights.

The Fae might not have the same kind of technology we had on earth, but they certainly weren't living in the Dark Ages.

Finally, we reached a massive domed room. Benches ringed the sides, and weapons hung high on the walls. The space was crowded with different species. At a glance, I saw witches, vampires, shifters, and mages. Not to mention quite a few Fae. The magical signatures in the room nearly bowled me over.

They were all trying to impress each other with how strong they were.

It kind of worked.

There was some serious competition in here.

I was good in a fight—really good—and I had a few magical skills I could call on. Transportation, amplification, seeker, the ability to send messages to someone's mind, as well as speed and strength. But the big guns—my Dragon Blood magic—couldn't be used in front of other people. I didn't need them figuring out what I was. Even using it just a little bit was a risk.

Even now, I could feel that I couldn't transport directly out of this realm. It was blocked. If I were caught spying on the king, it'd be nearly impossible to escape.

Nerves shivered along my skin, and I suppressed them. It wouldn't do to show weakness.

"Stay here," the guard growled. "They'll call for you soon enough."

"The games will begin soon, then?"

He nodded sharply, then turned and left.

I made a circle around the room, checking out my competition. On the far side, away from where I'd entered, there were arched cutouts in the wall. They revealed the hallway beyond, and a dozen competitors were crowded around, looking out.

I strolled over, catching their whispers.

"He's here!"

"That's him.'

"King Tarron."

Ooh, the king? Perfect.

I hurried forward, squeezing in between a guy who definitely smelled like a shifter and a woman who was likely a witch.

A group of Fae were walking down the hall toward us. The ones in the back were dressed in their finery, all gazing obsequiously at the figure in the front.

He strode along in a deep green suit—modern and from the human realm—his dark hair glinting in the fairy light.

I gasped and stumbled back.

Holy fates.

Holy fates.

The king was the same man who'd visited my shop.

The same one who knew I was a Dragon Blood.

The same one who thought I was his fated mate. And didn't like it.

5

MY HEART THUNDERED SO LOUD THAT IT NEARLY DEAFENED me. I spun away from the archways that led to the hallway and hurried in the opposite direction.

Oh, this was bad. So, so bad.

I bumped into a woman, who grunted and turned. "What's your problem?"

"Sorry. Bathroom. Where's the bathroom?"

"Nervous?" She raised a blue eyebrow, and her pink eyes softened. Her white wings glittered under the light.

"Uh, yeah. Where is it?'

She hiked a thumb toward some doors near the entrance. I hurried toward them, too distracted to even thank her. By the time I entered the bathroom, I was nearly panting.

Thank fates he hadn't seen me.

And thank fates the bathroom was empty. I didn't need a witness to my semi freak-out.

I stalked toward the sink basin. Public bathrooms in the Fae realm weren't dissimilar from ones in the human world, except for the fact that they were a hell of a lot nicer. Water poured continuously into blue crystal bowls. No water shortage here, apparently. The mirrors gleamed inside pale wooden frames made of beautifully twisted tree limbs.

I leaned over the basin of water, staring into the mirror and trying to get it together. Fates, I needed a cigarette. But that wasn't going to happen, so I shoved one of my old-lady candies into my mouth and sucked hard.

"This isn't over yet." I spoke to my reflection, feeling stupid but needing the lifeline.

My comms charm buzzed to life with magic, and Aeri's voice came through. "Mari? You all right?"

"Could you sense I was freaking out?"

"I don't know, maybe. What's wrong?"

"The man who knows what I am—he's the Fae king. He lied about his name and he's actually the Fae king."

"Shit. Get out of there."

"I can't."

"Of course you can."

"No. This job is important. You heard what Agatha said."

She didn't say anything, but I could almost see her scowling. "Let me do it. I can replace you in an hour."

"We don't have an hour. The games are about to start, and there'd be no way to get you here in time. You'd need a medallion to enter the Fae realm." And if it really was as dangerous as the little hobgoblin had said, I didn't want my sister competing.

Sure, she was immensely powerful, but she was still my sister. I couldn't live with it if she died in some crappy competition because of me.

And I *had* to do this. I had bigger reasons for coming here. And it'd been fine when I'd thought he was just some Fae.

As the king...

The one I was spying on....

I couldn't let him recognize me. It would complicate everything. I needed my answers first, then I'd deal with the rest.

But could I hide?

My reflection gazed back at me. Big hair, black eye makeup, and my tits half out because my zipper was partially pulled down.

So easily recognizable.

My disguise—which wasn't so much a disguise as one side of my personality—was so loud and in your face that a person wouldn't miss me coming. I hid in plain sight by being so visible they couldn't look away.

I reached up and rubbed at the eye makeup.

"Mari? What are you doing?" Aeri asked. "The silence is freaking me out."

"I've got a plan."

"What is it?"

"I'm going to hide what I am. But I need you to do something for me."

"Anything."

It was a long shot, but I had to ask. "Go to the bookshelf. See if there is a potion or spell for hiding a fated mate." ·

"A fated *what?*"

Quickly, I explained about the man. Who happened to be the king.

"Oh fates, Mari. You've gotten yourself into it this time."

"Seriously. Now just go look." I didn't know if he'd recognize something about me—my aura or something—or if touching me might trigger it, but I didn't need him recognizing me as his fated mate. That'd blow my cover as quick as anything.

"I'm on it. Hang on."

I cut the connection with the comms charm and dipped my hands under the running water.

Two minutes later, I was makeup free, my hair was slicked back into a sleek ponytail, and my top was zippered up almost to my neck.

No makeup, no hair, no tits.

Perfect. The king wouldn't even see me.

I looked totally different.

And I felt totally naked.

I drew in a shuddery breath. I hadn't gone out into the world without my disguise in years. Ever. It definitely made me look different.

I had to risk it. Because this was my opportunity to kill two birds with one stone. I'd figure out what the king was up to with the demon energy that filled this place, then I'd make him forget what I was—or I'd kill him.

"Mari?" Aeri's voice came through the line. "There's a potion. It'll create a mark on you but it should work. However, if he figures out who you are through other means, it will fail."

So I wouldn't let him find out. "Complicated ingredients?" I hadn't packed much in my bag that I'd stashed in the ether.

"No, normal stuff. The key is how you use them."

"Perfect. What is it?"

She explained the spell, then I hung up and got to work, taking the ingredients out of the ether. Thank fates I had them all.

As quickly as I could, I found the switch to turn the sink water off and plugged it up. My heart thundered as I mixed the ingredients in the basin, then dipped one of my knives into it. Once the blade was coated, I raised it to my chest. Slowly, I drew the blade down from the base of my throat to the start of my cleavage, leaving a shallow slice. Pain flared, and I embraced it.

A line of blood welled, and the potion seeped into my skin. I spoke the spell that Aeri had told me. "Hide me from his sight, his will and might. Forever free, my will it be."

Magic swirled around me and the wound on my throat glowed. The potion spread out across my skin, forming a swirling tattoo that was really quite beautiful. It disappeared inside my skin and the wound closed.

I shivered.

There. It should work.

I packed away my ingredients, cleaned the sink, then drew in one last breath and walked back out into the competitors' waiting area.

A pretty girl about my age stood near the door. She looked vaguely familiar, and I realized that it was the same one who'd given me directions to the bathroom. Now that I wasn't panicking, I got a good look at her. She had blue hair and pointed ears, along with pink eyes that were just slightly too big. Her wings were an ephemeral white.

A Fae from earth, if I had to guess. She didn't quite have the otherworldly glow of the Fae from this realm.

Her eyes ran up and down my form, lingering on my face. "Felt the need for a makeover?"

Shit, she'd noticed. "Wasn't working for me."

She stuck out her hand. "I'm Luna."

"Mari." It was weird to use my private name, but the king knew me as Mordaca, so I couldn't use that here. I nodded at her but didn't reach out. I wasn't really into touching. "Nice to meet you."

I strode away from her without another word. It wouldn't do to become attached to the other contestants.

I found a spot in the middle of the room and waited, sizing up my opponents. They did the same to me, and I felt naked without my mask.

"It is time!" The voice carried over the crowd of people, though I couldn't make out the source. "Advance to the arena."

Contestants began to flood back to the main doors through which we'd entered. Apparently they'd gotten some memo I hadn't, so I followed along.

We flowed out of the waiting area and into the night air. The sun had fully set and the sky was a deep midnight navy. Stars sparkled above, and night birds sang.

Luna joined my side. "We're headed to the arena now. It's huge apparently. Right behind the castle."

"Where'd you learn this?" I followed behind the supernaturals in front of me.

"Competitors meeting. Happened right before you came in."

"You noticed me come in?"

"Yeah, you looked like a sexy raincloud."

"Uh, thanks?"

"Not a compliment."

I laughed, liking her.

We walked alongside the castle wall, through the side courtyard, and out a massive gate on the west side. There had to be at least two dozen of us, and Fae guards surrounded us on all sides. They rode enormous winged stags like the ones that had pulled the carriage.

Every minute, it seemed like I sensed more demonic energy. In some places, it looked like a black fog rolling over the ground. It reeked of old cheese and fish, but no one else seemed to notice.

I nodded toward the guards. "I guess they don't want us wandering off in their realm, huh?"

"No." The girl sounded bitter.

"That's one of the reasons you came?"

"My mother took us from the Fae realm when we were kids. Not this one—another one in Norway—but I want to be with my own kind again."

"They won't have you back?"

"Not the Norse Fae. And these ones? Maybe if I win the competition."

"They're really secretive, aren't they?"

"Wouldn't you be, if you had a place like this to protect?"

I looked around, taking in the beautiful, ornate houses built of pale wood. The air smelled fresh and clean, and a faint sense of magic sparked in the sky. There was a general aura of contentment, if one ignored the slightest tinge of demonic energy that reeked of brimstone.

"Does this place smell a little funny to you?" I asked.

"No, it's amazing." She answered so quickly that I wasn't sure whether or not to believe her. "I could definitely live here. Couldn't you?"

"I don't know." I shrugged. "No cars. TV. Cell phones."

"I could do without all those things."

I couldn't. At least, I didn't want to give up my Mustang. Or my regular life. Especially not to live some weird enchanted one with a bunch of glowing Fae who were surrounded by demon energy that they didn't seem to notice.

Finally, we reached the arena.

"Whoa." The girl tilted her head back and looked up as we passed between two enormous trees.

"I do like the trees, though." I inspected the huge ring of them that created the arena.

It had to be the size of two or three football fields, with the huge redwoods shooting toward the sky. The branches grew over the arena to form a dome, and fairy lights sparkled among them, creating a blanket of light overhead.

High in the trees, viewing platforms nestled amongst the branches. Each one was filled with a Fae family, and it didn't take me long to find the king's platform.

He wasn't there, but it was the fanciest of the lot—built of the pale branches that were so common here. Silver ornamentation decorated it, twisting through the branches. A massive silver stag's head was mounted to the front of the platform, the horns curving up and around the back.

"He's into stags, huh?" I asked.

"All of these Fae are, not just him. Glorious creatures."

"Sure." I was more a dog and cat person, but I'd never met an animal I didn't like.

There was nothing inside the circular arena except grass. Around the edges were two dozen small platforms situated equal distances apart.

The girl pointed. "I bet we're supposed to stand on those."

From what I could tell, none had a tactical advantage over the other, so I chose the closest one and headed toward it, saying over my shoulder, "Good luck."

"You too."

The girl picked a platform farther away. I turned my attention to the rest of the contestants. There was a lion shifter with the trademark wild golden hair and cunning eyes. Something about the face was always distinct. It wasn't easy to recognize them, but I'd dated one for a while. A decent guy, besides the faint animal smell.

Next to him stood a vampire—that one would be fast. She had a slender, eerie beauty and long fangs that she didn't try to hide. They normally stayed up in the mouth when the vampire was trying to appear normal, but not this lady. She was ready to show the world what she was.

In fact, most of the people here were posturing. Trying to look tougher than they were. I preferred for people to underestimate me before a fight.

A gong sounded, loud and clear through the forest. Birds chirped and the fairy lights at the roof of the dome zipped around more quickly.

I looked up toward the king's platform. He was there.

Impassive, cold.

He looked just as he had when he'd come to my shop, only somehow more regal now. His bearing was straight and his shoulders broad. He was bigger than the figures who surrounded him, who weren't small either.

That had to be his Court.

There were at least eight of them, Fae of both sexes standing slightly behind him.

The king's gaze traveled over the contestants, bored.

If he'd seen me, I couldn't tell.

I watched, my breath held, as his gaze moved from platform to platform. When it finally fell on me, he tilted his head. My heart leapt into my throat and my skin chilled. Heat followed, the memory of the kiss blasting into my mind.

Shit.

Did he recognize me?

No. My makeup and hair went a long way toward disguising me. Not to mention my tits. He'd looked at those quite a bit, though subtly. I looked totally different now. And the spell was working. I'd seen the tattoo on my chest. Could feel it inside me. He couldn't sense that I was his *Mograh*.

Interest seemed to flicker in his gaze.

No. That had to be my imagination.

I looked away from him, determined not to show my interest.

At the top of the arena, a blue light glowed. A woman appeared, a beautiful Fae with pale blue and black hair. She floated high on gossamer wings of deep blue, her dress sweeping down around her form in a swirl of silk and sparkles. The glitter seemed to be made of light and magic. She lowered to the ground.

With a sweeping gesture, she spoke to the crowd. "Welcome to the Trials of the Fae. A competition of strength, wit, and magic that is sure to delight your senses. For the first time in five years, we gather together to watch the best of the supernatural world compete for glory and honor." She smiled. "And prizes."

Her gaze dropped to us, and she spun in a graceful circle as she spoke to the contestants. "You have come from all over the magical world to compete in a competition that will require the best of your magic, strength, and cunning. Some of you *will* die. Some will be maimed. Such is the cost of competing for the honor of victory within this realm. But if you win! Oh, if you win..." She smiled mysteriously, and I just wanted to shake her so she'd spit it out. "You will win the Wish Stone, an ancient carved stone ball that will grant you one single wish. *Anything* you desire will be yours, short of eternal life."

Hmm. Not a bad prize at all. I could use one of those. No wonder so many people were here. They'd have their greatest wish granted.

Maybe I could find the identity of my mother with it.

No. I'm fine without it.

I just needed to stop her; I didn't need to know her.

"Survival is only part of the competition," the Fae announcer said. "You will receive points for physical skill and showmanship—both with your daring and your magic."

Shit.

My magic wasn't that impressive.

Sure, I could create any kind of magic I wanted, but if anyone saw me do it, they'd know what I was.

I could *not* let that happen.

In a pinch, I could create temporary magic, but I'd have to *really* need it. Otherwise, my innate talents weren't all that showy. I could transport, amplify other magic, and appear as a vision inside someone's mind. Not to mention my slight seeker sense and increased speed and strength. But none of that was the flash-bang stuff that got you extra points in a competition like this. The only cool-looking power that I had was my ability to make a lightning whip that joined with Aeri's. Without her, I couldn't do it.

So I'd just have to be clever. And daring.

Done and done.

The Fae announcer floated a bit higher into the air to make sure that she had everyone's attention. "Because of the risks involved in such a competition, we request that you sign your life away."

Huh. Even the Fae were afraid of litigation.

A heavy piece of parchment appeared in the air in front of me, along with an impressive quilled pen. The glowing text on the paper was minimal.

Should I die during the Trials of the Fae, I vow that I will not haunt this realm or seek vengeance for my death. Nor shall my family, friends, or acquaintances.

Well, I couldn't speak for Aeri, but it wasn't like I was going to not sign and not compete. This wasn't any more dangerous than my real life. Hell, just by being born as a Dragon Blood, I'd pretty much signed my life away to a gruesome death one day.

But I didn't want to sign my real name. They might be

able to track me with that. And if the king really was that interested in me...

I glanced up at his box, trying to be subtle.

His gaze was still on me.

Shit. Double shit.

I picked up the pen and started to sign another name —Elizabeth Keane. But the pen wouldn't move.

Ohhhh, tricky Fae.

Tricky, tricky.

I tried a second fake name just to be sure—Katherine Torrence. The pen glowed red.

Crap. It was going to tell on me.

Hastily I scribbled my real name. Mari.

The pen glided smoothly.

Well, that was bad news.

Hopefully the king wouldn't inspect the contract. He might not even know me as Mari—Mordaca was my public name, after all.

After I signed, the pen and paper disappeared. I looked up.

The announcer grinned widely, raising her hands high above her head. "Your first challenge will be to collect as many glowing prizes as you can." She held out her hand, and a goblet appeared, hovering over her palm. It glowed with a golden light. "And remember, showmanship counts! So if you want to make it to the next round, be entertaining."

There was a rumble of excitement through the crowd. I shifted, getting ready for whatever was to come.

Survive. Big magic. Get points.

"And let the games begin!" She rose up toward the trees, spinning as she went. Her hand swept low by her side, magic flowing from her fingertips. The arena in front of me filled with trees and plants, then with a few ponds and rock outcroppings. The people in the stands still had a good view because they were up high, but down here, there was plenty of cover and terrain to work with.

Then the monsters came.

First, I heard the roar.

A half second later, an enormous beast appeared in the middle of the arena. It was a wolf-like creature, with black spikes for fur.

To the left, three banshees appeared. They hovered in midair, their ragged dresses floating around their ephemeral forms. Black hair hung in their faces, and their eyes glowed with a blazing fury. They shrieked, and I slapped my hands to my ears.

Banshee cries came before death.

They were announcing it.

It was a given that one of us would die here. Maybe more.

On the other side of the arena, a huge tree monster grew up from the ground. It was made of pieces of wood all bound together with vines and moss. Long pointed claws tipped each finger, and fangs descended from the mouth. It had to be at least ten feet tall.

A dozen other monsters appeared, all different sizes

and shapes. The scent of dark magic filled the air—like rotten milk left out in the sun and then mixed with tuna fish and flour to create the most disgusting cake ever made.

Some of these monsters—like the banshees—were probably real and had come here for the fun of it. Others were creations of black magic that weren't truly living. They could fight like they were, though, with all the ferocity of a demon.

My gaze ran over them all, and I calculated the ways I could kill them.

Throughout the landscape, gold began to glow. The prizes. They were stuck in trees and on top of rock outcroppings, submerged in the ponds and even floating in the air.

Okay, I had to survive the monsters and the other contestants and grab as many of those suckers as I could.

Easy peasy.

Tension thrummed, vibrating against my skin.

It was about to begin.

And I had eyes for only one monster.

The biggest of them all. I'd only ever seen one in books, but there was no doubt about this creature. An underworld wurm—like a horned snake and a demon had a baby. The creature was at least fifty feet tall, a serpent with four legs that dragged its belly low to the ground. Its neck and head loomed high overhead, thirty feet up and swaying like a cobra ready to strike.

The eyes were flame red and the enormous fangs

dripped with green venom. Spikes decorated the entire spine. A golden gem sat in its head.

That was the prize I wanted.

I needed points, and taking him down was the best way to get them.

The bell sounded, and I charged.

6

THE CROWD ROARED AS THE CONTESTANTS RACED TOWARD the monsters. Their cries of delight echoed through the arena, and pieces of colorful confetti rained down upon my head.

Blood-thirsty bastards.

I narrowed my eyes on the huge, serpentine beast that slithered along the ground, head waving thirty feet in the air. I was the only one who headed for the underworld wurm.

Good.

I drew my bow and arrow from the ether. It was one of my favorite weapons, and I was good with it. I raised it and aimed for the left eye. I nocked the arrow and fired, hitting on the first try.

The creature didn't even shriek in pain—monsters made of dark magic rarely felt anything. It made them even more formidable. But it thrashed its head, trying to dislodge the arrow that ruined its vision. I could go for the second eye, but I'd probably get more points if this were difficult. So I didn't even try.

Showmanship was the name of the game here, and boy, was I going to give them a show.

I flourished my bow as I stashed it back in the ether and raced forward. The wurm recovered enough to stop thrashing. It swung its head around, searching for whoever had done it wrong.

"Hey, big fella!" I shouted and raised my arms. "I'm over here!"

And I hoped I was as fast as I thought I was.

The creature hissed and struck, its head shooting for me. I used my magic, transporting to a spot behind the serpent's head. I sprinted alongside the massive body supported by four squat legs.

The creature raised its head, searching for me, but I didn't give it a chance. I headed for one leg and used it to climb up the serpent's back. I raced alongside the ridge of spikes that lined the creature's back, hanging on to them whenever the serpent tried to buck me off.

All around, the crowd roared. Somehow, I could feel the heat of the king's gaze on me.

He couldn't possibly recognize me though. I had to believe that.

I caught brief glimpses of contestants facing off against other monsters. Then I began to climb. I used the spikes like a ladder, scrambling up to the top of the monster's head. It thrashed, trying to throw me off, but I clung tightly.

One aggressive shudder had me hanging from a spike with no foothold. I swung my body, managing to catch a second spike with my foot, and climbed higher. When I reached the head, I gripped a spike with one hand and drew my sword from the ether with the other.

Wind tore at my hair as the beast tried to shake me off. Dark magic welled from the beast. I raised my sword and gripped it with both hands, then plunged it into his skull. The blade pierced cleanly, and the creature roared.

It thrashed, going down hard. I yanked my blade free and leapt off, then rolled to safety. Pain flared in my knee when I hit the ground wrong, but I ignored it and surged upright, just in time to see the monster explode in a poof of black magic.

A single glowing gem lay in the middle of the arena, right where his body had been. I sprinted for it, then scooped it up and shoved it into my pocket. It glowed warmly, magic tingling up my thigh.

Panting, I swung around, looking for my next opponent. My next prize.

I spared the king one glance—still watching—then turned my attention to the arena. All around me was chaos. Monsters fighting contestants, blades flashing, and magic exploding. A fire mage shot a huge ball of flame at a banshee while the vampire tore out the throat of a green-skinned ogre. A stallion with a flaming mane galloped around the arena, breathing fire on anyone who got too near.

There were monsters of all realms in here, not just the Fae or Celtic. Apparently the king had gone all out for this and brought in an arsenal.

Right in the middle of the arena was a blackthorn tree. The midnight bark was spiked and rough, the leaves a dark, glossy green. In the middle of the branches, another golden object glowed. A small circle of metal. A wolf-like creature prowled in front of it, black smoke wafting around its spiked body. It wasn't built of flesh and blood, but rather spikes from the tree.

The Lunatisidhe. The mythical protector of the blackthorn tree, a creature of Scottish legend.

It had to be important to the Fae.

Definitely worth a lot of points.

But the menace that emanated from the thorn wolf made my blood chill.

The wurm had been big and mean, but this guy would be fast and vicious.

Even more importantly—I probably shouldn't kill it.

Trees and nature were vital to the Fae, and this wolf was the sacred protector of one of the most valuable trees.

So it was super dangerous, *and* I shouldn't kill it.

No wonder no one had gone after this monster yet.

He's mine.

I sprinted for it, dodging a wrestling pair of contestants who were fighting over a glowing golden crown.

They'd lose points for that, I'd bet.

As if it sensed my approach over the noise of the battle, the wolf turned to me and growled. It lowered its head, muzzle pulled back from fangs. Powerful magic radiated from the creature. Unlike the wurm, the signature wasn't dark. But it was powerful. The creature's magic smelled like a cold morning mist and felt like rough bark beneath my fingertips. One eye glowed, the other was missing.

I called upon my potion bag from the ether. Before I could draw a bomb out, the monster shot a big black thorn right off its back. The spike flew through the air, hurtling toward me. Heart thundering, I dived left, narrowly avoiding the projectile.

A shriek sounded from behind me.

I glanced back, horrified.

Had it hit another contestant?

Not the girl I'd spoken to, I prayed.

Behind me, a banshee clutched the thorn that pierced her through the stomach.

Thank fates.

She'd be fine. It'd probably just piss her off more.

I turned back to the thorn wolf. It crouched lower, shooting another spike.

I lunged to the right, grateful for my speed, and called upon my shield from the ether. The metal and wooden contraption appeared in my hand, and I held it up, blocking the next three thorns that slammed into the metal.

I crept closer, awkwardly clutching my potion bag and digging around inside for the sedative. I didn't often use potions like this and was slow, but I finally grabbed the distinctive triangular vial.

As I neared the wolf, I got a better sense of its magic, and damn, was this guy powerful.

I was only about thirty feet away now. I peeked around the shield, calling upon my amplification magic. This power allowed me to increase the oomph of any magic around me.

I fed it into the sedative bomb, which was a glittering red liquid. My power flowed into the glass vial, making it glow. Then I hurled the glass at the wolf, trying to shove even more of my amplification magic toward the crimson bomb that flew through the air.

The glass exploded against the wolf's side. A burst of glittering red magic surged upward, a mushroom cloud of scarlet sparkles that filled the top of the dome. The crowd oohed and ahhed.

One of the flying monsters—a two-headed crow—got caught in the blast and plummeted to the ground, unconscious.

I sprinted for the scarlet cloud and the wolf that lay within. As I neared, I slowed just slightly. I didn't want to get caught in the sedative haze before it dissipated or I'd be unconscious too.

Talk about embarrassing, getting hit with your own potion bomb.

The cloud faded away, and I approached the tree. The branches dipped low, spikey and black. They seemed to be curving toward the fallen wolf, who lay unconscious beneath the limbs.

He'd be out for a while, probably.

The sound of the battle echoed behind me. What if some idiot tried to kill him to get points without realizing how important he was?

Shit.

I hadn't thought of that.

I crept farther beneath the canopy of blackthorn limbs that hung overhead, my gaze on the wolf. When the tree didn't shoot any spikes at me, I stashed my shield in the ether. The wolf's thorny coat was still surrounded in a black misty haze. I probably shouldn't touch him with my skin, but I couldn't leave him here.

Shit. What should I do?

The tree was clearly trying to protect the wolf, but the limbs couldn't reach it.

Thinking quickly, I slipped my hands back in my sleeves so that they were covered with leather, then I crept over to the wolf and reached down to grab its black foot.

I heaved it toward the tree trunk, dragging the unconscious body.

"Damn, you're heavy, pal." I grunted and heaved, finally reaching the trunk.

I pushed the wolf's unconscious body up against the trunk. Immediately, the bark grew outward, encapsulating the wolf.

I grinned. "Well, that worked nicely."

"It did indeed."

The cool, deep voice sent a frisson of terror down my

spine. It cut through the sound of battle clearly and cleanly.

Without turning, I knew exactly who it was.

Tarron.

The king.

I swallowed hard and turned.

The king stood beneath the branches of the blackthorn tree, his suit impeccably cut and perfect. It did nothing to hide the warrior's body and stance, however. He'd had this look about him when he'd arrived on my doorstep, but not so extreme.

Here, he looked almost feral.

Like being in the Fae realm turned him into his truest self. He was revealed, and the clothes did nothing to hide it.

His green eyes watched me closely, curiously.

I shivered. "Shouldn't you be up in your box? Watching?"

He pointed toward it. "I am."

I looked up at the box. His body stood there, looking exactly the same as before. Except he wasn't moving much. His gaze was still on the crowd below.

"Whoa." I looked back down at the king, realizing that his form wasn't quite opaque. "Astral projection?"

He nodded.

Cool. It was a bit like what I could do—appearing in someone's mind. But he appeared in the world.

"How did you know that weapons would only make the wolf stronger?" he asked.

"What do you mean?"

"A sword blow gives him strength, an acid bomb makes him faster. Flame will make him grow. But you hit him with the only thing that would weaken him. Kindness."

My brows rose, and I looked down at the wolf, who was now almost entirely absorbed back into the tree. He was the perfect fighting machine. Almost.

"I just hit him with a sedative," I said.

"Like I said. Kindness. You chose not to kill him."

"He was just protecting the tree. I wasn't going to kill him."

"You killed the wurm."

"Not really. The wurm was made of magic. I just destroyed it."

He inclined his head, looking almost confused. Impossibly handsome. Definitely intrigued. "You are interesting. Almost familiar."

I shrugged, nerves lighting up throughout my body. "What I am is busy." I pointed to the golden bracelet still nestled among the tree branches. "I need to collect that prize, then go get some more."

I turned from him, hoping he would get the hint. I needed to learn more about him. But right now, I needed to ensure I stayed in the competition.

Carefully, I approached the tree. This thing still had plenty of spikes that it could shoot at me, but it didn't seem inclined, thank fates.

When I neared the trunk, I spared a glance at the space behind me.

The king was gone.

Was he appearing to other contestants like this?

Somehow, I had a feeling that he wasn't.

I turned back to the tree, drawing in a deep breath. The challenge wasn't over yet. The bracelet was encapsulated in a ring of thorns that would shred my hand—and probably poison me—if I reached inside. Carefully, I laid my palm against the bark.

The magic within the tree reminded me of the protective spells that guarded the Well of Power beneath my house.

I closed my eyes and focused on my intentions.

I won't hurt you. I won't hurt the wolf.

I repeated the mantra, adding in *please give me the bracelet.*

After a few seconds, the magic in the tree diminished. Almost as if it were drawing back into itself. I looked at the bracelet. The thorns were pulling back, revealing the gold within.

Quickly, I reached up and snagged it.

"Thank you." I slipped the glowing golden circle around my wrist and turned from the tree.

I gave the wolf one last look, barely able to see him where he was protected within the trunk, then stepped toward the battle that still raged outside.

A shriek sounded from above.

My heart lunged into my throat, and I looked up.

Too late.

A massive, icy blue bird was plunging toward me, so

fast I couldn't even move. The creature grabbed me in its claws, picking me up and tucking me under its body. It bound my arms to my sides, its huge talons gripping me around the chest.

Freezing cold surged through me where the bird touched me. The whole creature was made of ice. It had a grip on my arms that bound me from reaching for my weapons. I shuddered hard, cold freezing my veins.

I tried moving my head, hoping to get a better look and find a weak spot, but my neck could barely move. All of me felt cold and stiff, and the only thing I could see was icy feathers.

Shit. What was this creature?

All around, the crowd roared. Below, contestants and monsters lay sprawled on the ground. At least half were dead or grievously wounded. More than half of the monsters were gone as well.

I'd be gone soon, too, if I didn't think of something quick. With every second, more coldness stole through my veins, leaching out my strength. Even my mind moved more slowly.

Think. Think.

I called upon my transportation magic, trying to zap myself out of the bird's grasp. A sensation of tearing exploded in my chest, and I gasped, pain shooting through me.

Yeah, that didn't work.

Head pounding, mind racing, I settled on the only answer.

My Dragon Blood.

If my current magic wouldn't get me out of this, I needed new magic. I couldn't just blast out of this bird's grip. We were a hundred feet over the ground. A fall would kill me. Maim me, at least.

I had to weaken him. And what weakened ice but fire?

I drew in a steady breath and carefully sliced my thumb with my sharp fingernail. Dragon Blood magic was tricky. If I wanted to make a lot of magic—or a new permanent magical skill—I needed a *lot* of blood.

But a little new magic? Temporary magic?

That took just a little blood. And secrecy. Always secrecy.

I kept my hand hidden by my thigh as my black blood welled. I wiped it onto my black pants—an extra handy color for me—and called upon my magic. As my blood flowed, my power welled within me.

I could try my suggestive magic, but that hadn't worked on the Fae king and I couldn't be guaranteed it would work on the bird either.

I envisioned the new magic that I wanted to have— something that I'd never seen another mage possess.

I imagined heating up from the inside like an iron. I would be a human torch. The magic sparked within my veins, filling me up and surging out of me. Warmth flowed through me, turning to heat.

The bird shuddered, and its grip loosened.

Shit.

I had just enough room to wiggle, so I grabbed onto

the bird's talons. My legs dangled as the bird slackened its grip on me. I clung tightly, feeding more of the heat into the bird. I smeared my black blood onto its icy blue leg, forcing my warmth into it. Feeding it my magic and my heat.

The icy wings flapped slower, and then dipped lower in the air. We floated right in front of the king's platform. I caught a glimpse of his green gaze as I turned my head away, panic fluttering in my chest.

He always seemed to be watching me. *Always.*

I called my magic into me, making sure that my signature didn't flare too brightly. The last thing I needed was the king realizing what I was doing.

Especially since he knew about Dragon Bloods. I didn't think he'd made the connection that I was the same woman he'd met, but it was still too close for comfort.

Finally, the bird was close enough to the ground that I wouldn't die if I fell. I forced a blast of heat into him, strong enough that he melted in a rush of water that poured over my head and drenched me like a tidal wave. I slammed onto the ground, gasping.

Out of the corner of my eye, I caught sight of another golden gem sitting in a puddle. It had been inside the bird, and now it sat only five yards from me.

A bit farther away, the lion shifter sprinted toward the gem. He was in full lion form, his massive mane blowing in the wind and his fur golden and bright. His keen yellow eyes were glued to the prize.

"Bastard!" I scrambled to my feet. No way I'd let this opportunistic feline steal my treasure.

I raced for the gem, swooping it up right before the lion reached it. His huge body plowed into mine and knocked me to the ground. He loomed over me, fangs gleaming.

Then his head plunged downward as he went for my throat.

I burst into action, adrenaline and instinct driving me. I rolled to the side as his fangs slammed down. They tore through my upper arm and pain flared. I shrieked.

This bastard was going to kill me.

7

PANTING, I BROUGHT MY FEET UP AND KICKED THE LION SO hard in the stomach that he flew off me. I scrambled upright and shoved the gem into my pocket.

The lion roared and surged to his feet, charging me.

Bastard.

Instead of fighting a monster for a gem, he'd decided that I was easy prey.

"Wrong, sucker," I growled as I drew a dagger from the ether.

I had three prizes right now, and they'd all stay mine, no matter how badly he wanted them.

He leapt toward me, and I dived right, slamming my dagger into his side. I yanked it sideways, then pulled it out.

He roared and turned on me, blood pouring from his side.

"I'm not going to kill you," I said, dancing to the right to avoid him. "I'm just going to embarrass you."

The lion lunged for me, and I darted away again. This time I was too slow, and he sliced a claw on the side of my thigh. Agony shot through me, and I stumbled.

"Oh, I'm losing patience." I hurtled toward him and slammed my blade into his leg. I sliced hard and deep, and he roared.

I pulled my blade back and scrambled away. He went down hard, his back leg out for the count.

Aching, I stood. Blood poured from my thigh and arm, but not enough to stop me. Fortunately, it blended with my black clothes so no one could see that I was weird. The lion shifter roared and dragged himself toward me with his front legs. If he'd been a real cat, I'd have felt guilty as hell.

But I could still remember him as a man, standing on that platform with his cunning eyes, analyzing the contestants.

To see which of us he'd take out.

Not me.

"I'm done with you." I darted away, not interested in killing another contestant.

I had enough blood on my hands. I'd stick to demons and black magic apparitions, thanks very much.

A scream sounded from behind me. I spun, spotting the blue-haired Fae in the grip of two banshees. They were trying to tear her apart, their skeletal grip tight on her arms.

"Oh, hell," I muttered, then sprinted for them.

I limped, but I was still fast. I reached the closest banshee without her hearing me, and grabbed her around the neck, yanking her away from the Fae.

The icy touch of death seeped from her skin, into my hands and up my arms. My wounds burned more fiercely as cold swept through my veins. Aching, I threw the banshee away from me, and the creature whirled, rising up on the air like a terrifying witch. Her ragged black hair hung in her face, and her black eyes burned with evil intent.

"You're one creepy bitch, you know that?" I drew my sword from the ether. "The fact that you're levitating without wings is...yikes."

She howled, her mouth a great gaping black hole.

"You're joking if you think that shriek foretells my death," I said.

Her eyes burned into me, and she flew toward me, arms outstretched. She was almost upon me when I swung, going right for her skinny white neck. Her head tumbled off and bounced on the ground with her ragged hair flying. The body dropped hard to the grass, then disappeared in a poof of black dust.

Unlike the ice bird, her body didn't contain a gem. She wasn't really a prize—just an obstacle.

Ten yards away, the Fae slammed her blue dagger into the other banshee's eye.

"Got it under control?" I shouted.

"With delight." She twisted the blade.

I spun in a circle, looking for more prizes. More threats.

Most of the monsters were down. Many of the contestants too. Only one gem was left. It sat at the top of a slender marble pedestal that rose thirty feet into the air.

No one had gone for it yet—not even the winged contestants.

That wasn't a great sign.

Whatever. I could take it. I sprinted for the pedestal. My stomach turned from the pain of each step, and I vowed to beat the shit out of the lion shifter again if he survived this round. Bastard.

As I neared the pedestal, dark magic rolled toward me. It smelled like flop sweat and felt like sadness. Like grief. Memories assailed me. I nearly doubled over as dark visions of my past filled my head.

Grimrealm. Aunt. Uncle.

No.

No. No. No.

I was the master of my mind, and my past would stay where I'd put it.

I drew in a ragged breath and sprinted forward, then finally reached the pedestal. There were tiny handholds cut into the stone. I just had to climb.

No big deal.

Except I was sweating and cold from the memories that swirled in my head.

Being locked in the dark room, wondering if they were hurting Aeri.

Hunger.

Beatings. Even worse, watching them beat Aeri.

Aunt forcing me to create new magic, threatening to tell Aeri what I really was if I didn't obey. Threatening to take her from me with the truth.

Not only was I remembering—I was feeling. Whatever spell they'd put on this challenge, it sent me right back to my worst memories so I lived them again.

Bile rose in my throat.

If I climbed this pedestal, it would only get worse.

I couldn't do it.

But did I have enough prizes to continue on in the competition? I couldn't fail, or they'd kick me out of this realm and I'd never learn about my mother. Worse, the dark magic could continue to spread and take over the entire kingdom. Then it would move to earth.

That was *so* not an option.

I hadn't seen any more prizes, which meant this was probably the last one.

With a shaking hand, I reached for the first divot in the marble. I touched the cold stone, and my head nearly tore apart from the pain. Every bad feeling I'd ever experience surged through me. And considering how I'd spent the first fifteen years of my life, that was some *bad shit.*

I yanked my hand away, tears smarting my eyes.

No.

I grabbed the handhold and hauled myself up. Then up higher. Pain nearly crippled me, memories tearing my mind apart. Ragged breaths filled my lungs as I forced myself to climb. But with every new handhold, things got worse.

Soon, I couldn't tell where I was.

Was I climbing out of the hole Aunt and Uncle had once put me in?

Yes, that was it. I was trying to escape that hole.

Except I never had. It had been too deep, and I had been too weak. Weak from the beatings, weak from hunger.

My mind spun. I had to let go. I had to fall. Go to sleep.

Blackness crept in at the edges of my vision.

No.

A low growl sounded from beneath me.

Instead of scaring me, it drove away some of the darkness.

The growl sounded again. This time louder.

More of the darkness receded.

I was no longer in the hole. I never had been. At least not today. No, I was climbing the pedestal at the Trials of the Fae. I was competing.

My head felt clearer.

The growl sounded a third time, and I looked down.

The thorn wolf. His side was pressed against the pedestal and his single eye was on me. His muzzle wasn't drawn back, and he didn't look threatening.

Strangely, I could feel his magic.

What the hell was happening?

Was he helping me?

Somehow, his magic seemed to be fighting the dark

spell that surrounded the pedestal and put my worst memories in my mind. I could feel his intentions.

Holy fates.

"Thanks," I whispered, then turned back to the pedestal and kept climbing.

Hand over hand, I moved as fast as I could. I didn't want to be caught up there if the dark magic returned.

I reached the top and grabbed the stone, then clambered back down as quickly as I could. As soon as I reached the ground, the thorn wolf disappeared.

All around, there was silence.

While I'd been reliving my own nightmares, the last of the monsters had been slayed. Most of the bodies were disappearing, though not all. Contestants stood scattered around the ring, covered in blood and burns, all of their faces painted with shocked expressions.

Holy fates, the Fae announcer hadn't been kidding.

We would die.

Many of us had. Most were grievously injured.

Jesus.

These Fae didn't mess around.

I heaved out a breath, clutching my prize. My gaze moved to the king. How could he allow this to happen? This was their idea of fun?

His gaze was riveted to me, and ice filled my veins. He'd watched me climb the pedestal. Had he seen me crying from my memories?

The idea horrified me to my core.

To the world, I was Mordaca. Sophisticated, supremely

self-collected Mordaca. I didn't show emotion. To anyone. Hardly even to Aeri.

And I'd cried in front of all these people. Cried in front of *him.*

Disgusted, I dragged my gaze to the right, away from him.

The Fae announcer appeared high above, her beautiful wings sparkling against the dark night sky. She didn't bother to land on the ground this time—probably didn't want to get her dress dirty. Something that the Mordaca side of me could relate to. I wouldn't step in this cesspool of blood and magic if I were wearing my good clothes either.

"Contestants, you have done well." Her gaze traveled over all of us. "Given your performances, only four of you shall pass on to the next round, which will commence tomorrow morning."

The crowd cheered, as if thrilled at the idea of more carnage.

"But there is only one winner today. One person collected the most prizes by far." Her gaze turned to me and she pointed. "Mari, the woman in black. You have collected four prizes. You will continue on. The other three contestants—each of whom managed two prizes—are Warrick the lion shifter, Luna the Fae, and Cardin the Mage. The rest of the contestants will be returning to their realm."

I passed.

The crowd cheered, but I didn't hear them. It took all I had just to stay on my feet.

As it turned out, winning did have its perks. I got my own chamber, and the healer visited me first. The slender Fae man with pale hair and blue eyes mended my wounds using magic, then left me alone to bathe in an amazing bathroom. It was the biggest bathroom I'd ever been in, complete with a submerged pool filled with warm water and opalescent bubbles.

This Fae realm was one of contrasts—gruesome battles and unimaginable splendor. The room alone was as big as my apartment at home, with fresh flowers blooming all along the borders and birds singing on the windowsill.

Once I was sure I was alone, I pressed my fingertip to my comms charm and ignited the magic, then whispered, "Aeri?"

"Mari!" Aeri whispered back. She knew that if I whispered when I called her, she needed to whisper right back.

"Don't speak. Just listen." I didn't know what spies were in the walls. "Call off your search. I've found what you're looking for."

"What? Really?"

"Yes."

"Ohhhh." I could tell she was desperate to ask questions, but she was smart enough not to. I gave her a quick update on the contest, but said nothing that I wouldn't want the king himself to hear.

"Well, be careful," Aeri said.

"I will. I promise." I cut the call and stared at the ceiling.

Damn, this place had me on edge. What I wouldn't give for a cigarette.

But nope. That was for past me.

Didn't stop me from wanting one all the same.

I sighed and climbed out of the water, then wrapped a fuzzy warm towel around myself.

At some point while the healer had been mending my wounds, a tiny figure with green skin and a long nose had come in to take my clothes for laundering. I hated to let them out of my sight, but there was no way for me to refuse without being suspiciously weird.

The bedroom that they'd assigned me was on the bottom floor of the castle. As I'd understood it, all of the contestants were down here somewhere. The room was large with a high ceiling. Sparkling water flowed down the walls and gave the room a fresh scent. The bed in the middle was large and plush, and it was like sleeping inside a waterfall.

I found a silky white robe—Aeri's color, not mine—and slipped it on, then walked toward the bed. I was feeling surprisingly fit after the healer's efforts. Which was good, since I needed to figure out how to sneak into the king's quarters tonight. This was just the opportunity I'd been waiting for.

"Hello?" a voice sounded from the door behind me.

I turned as the door opened.

The blue-haired Fae that I'd saved stood in the doorway. Luna. "Can I come in?"

I shrugged. "You already opened the door without knocking, so you might as well."

"I wanted to thank you for saving me." She strode in and stopped in front of me. She was still dressed in her fight wear. "Why'd you do it?"

I blinked at her blunt tone. "Um, didn't want you to be torn apart by banshees?"

"Why?"

"Because that would suck."

"Yeah. But not for you."

"Well, I certainly wouldn't have liked it." I studied her, wondering what kind of shitty life she'd led if she thought it was crazy that I'd saved her. I mean, my life had contained some sucky moments, but at least I'd always had Aeri. Deep in my bones, I had the knowledge that there was someone on earth who would die for me. That was worth a hell of a lot. "Don't worry about it."

"But I *am* worried about it. What do you want in return?"

"Um..." My mind raced. "Nothing, really."

There was something I wanted actually, but I didn't want to play it too eager.

"Come on. There's got to be something." She pulled a beautiful dagger out of the sheath at her thigh. The blade was wickedly sharp, and the hilt made of twisted silver and gems. "How about this? It's worth a ton, and then we'll be even."

Her life was worth more than a dagger, but I didn't want to go all Dr. Phil on her by trying to explain that.

"How about some info?" I said. "About this place."

"What about it?" She gestured around. "Clearly it's awesome."

"The king. What do you know about the king?"

"Ooh, that hottie, huh?"

"Yeah, super hot." And he *was*. Which was the perfect thing to throw her off the real reason for my inquiry. "I wouldn't mind getting to know him a bit better."

"Got a thing for royalty, huh?"

"Well, Prince Harry's taken, so I think the next best thing might be a Fae king."

She laughed. "I'm not sure you want this one." Her gaze turned serious. "Sure, he's hot. But he's got a sketchy past. Some say evil."

"How so?"

"He usurped the throne from his brother."

"Usurped?" My stomach pitched. "As in, violently?"

"Killed his brother in cold blood."

"Oh, fuck." I sat down on the bed. Images of Aeri flashed in my mind. He'd killed his own sibling. I couldn't imagine anything worse.

Was that the source of the torture I'd sensed in him when I'd done the spell yesterday?

I mean, who wouldn't be torn up about killing their

own sibling? Even an asshole would probably feel pretty guilty.

I raised my head and met Luna's gaze. "He must have really wanted the throne, huh?"

"That's the weird thing. People rarely see him, and he never looks happy. He's not holding court like a Fae normally would, not participating in revelry."

Participating in revelry had to be a Fae term for *partying.*

I frowned. "You'd think if he went to all the trouble to kill his way to the throne, he'd at least enjoy it. Why didn't the Fae overturn him?"

"It's not technically illegal as long as you're a blood relation. It's still frowned upon, though. Even though it's legal, it's one of those ancient laws the Fae don't like. Not very honorable, if you ask me."

"Shit, these Fae are intense."

"No kidding."

"You sure you want to be part of this? I don't think I'd risk death to join these weirdos."

"Normally it's pretty great, from what I hear."

Except for the fact that this place was plagued with demon energy. I could feel it even now, despite the beauty of the room. Did it have anything to do with brother killing brother?

Damn, I needed to figure this out. The deeper I got, the worse it became.

"Thanks for the info," I said. "I think I'll hold off on my pursuit."

"Smart. Still going to try to win?"

"Yeah."

"Well, I'll try to return the favor."

"If a banshee is tearing me apart?"

"Banshee, vampire, whatever. Good for one rescue."

"Thanks." I wasn't going to turn that down. She didn't seem that tough, but you never could tell.

"I'll leave you to it." She waved and turned to go.

Luna was gone for only a few minutes before there was another knock on the door. This person was polite enough to wait for me to open it.

Another woman stood on the other side, but I'd never seen her before. She was short and slight, with pink hair and green eyes. She held a swatch of bright blue silk draped over her arm.

My gaze moved from it to her. "Yes?"

"The king requests that you join him."

Well, shit.

That wasn't the sneaking around that I'd been hoping to do. "I'm still recovering."

"You look fine." Her eyes traveled up and down. "And declining is not an option."

No, it probably wasn't, if this guy was willing to kill his brother to get to the throne.

Memories of our kiss, of what I'd felt during the spell, assailed me. He was a bastard, yes. I wouldn't argue that. But I hadn't sensed *murderer* on him. And in a life like mine, you got pretty good at sensing murderers.

"All right, then." I gestured to the dress. "Is that for me?"

"It is." She handed it over.

I took it, enjoying the feel of silk beneath my hands. I only spent about ten percent of my life in my fight wear, hunting demons. The rest of the time I was Mordaca, silk-wearing, perfectly done-up Mordaca.

It hadn't felt natural when I'd first adopted the look. The disguise.

But I'd grown to love it.

Who wouldn't like wearing silk and looking like a scary, sexy Elvira?

I certainly liked it.

With the gown in my hands, I strode into the room and turned away from the woman. I dropped my robe and pulled the gown over my head. It floated around me, smooth, silken perfection. The sleeves were long and tight, and the skirt flared around my ankles.

I smoothed my hands over my front and looked down, catching sight of a good portion of my cleavage.

That wouldn't do.

The king had seen too much of me already. I didn't need to jog his memory.

I turned back to the woman, who was watching me with impassive eyes. I pointed to my breasts. "This has to change. I don't ever show this much skin."

Aeri would have laughed at that.

The woman lifted a hand and waved it in front of me.

Blue sparkles drifted from her fingers, and the neckline of the dress rose to almost my collarbones.

I raised my arms, showing her the long sleeves. They were too much like my Mordaca dress, even though the color was different. "These are too long."

She waved her hand again, and the sleeves were replaced by bands of fabric that covered just the corners of my shoulders. I looked down at the skirt. It was fine. Full and sparkly, without the slit that my usual dress possessed. That one revealed a good bit of thigh.

"Shoes?" I asked.

She held up her hand, and a drool-worthy pale of sparkly blue platform heels appeared. I wanted to grab them.

Instead, I frowned. "I only wear flats."

Aeri would have laughed again. But the five inches of height that my normal heels gave me was a lot. Being shorter would go a long way toward hiding me.

The Fae frowned and created some sparkly flats. They weren't bad, actually. I took them and slipped them on, feeling a bit weird. My heels were enchanted to be comfortable, so this wasn't even an upgrade in that sense.

"Hair and makeup?" I asked. I might as well do this disguise up right.

"Vain, aren't you?"

"Of course." I gestured to myself. "Look at me. Wouldn't you be?"

She scowled, then her face smoothed out. She conjured a box and handed it to me.

I took it and turned to the bathroom. "Be out in a bit."

It didn't take long to do my makeup. I kept it simple and vastly different than normal. Pale pink lips, absolutely no black makeup, and simple, sleek hair.

It wasn't a bad look, actually. But it wasn't me.

All the same, with the clothes, the height, and the makeup, I didn't look anything like Mordaca.

I snapped the makeup box shut and returned to the room. "All right. I'm ready to meet the king."

8

THE FAE WOMAN LED ME UP THROUGH THE CASTLE, AND I memorized every detail as we walked. On the plus side, there were a lot of windows. They gave exceptional views of the starry night sky and allowed a sweet breeze to flow through the open spaces. They'd be good escape options if I needed them.

On the downside, there were a lot of Fae. They roamed the halls, some seeming aimless as they walked. As if they just liked hanging out there.

"Who are these people?" I asked.

"Members of the Court and their friends."

"They just like hanging out around the king?"

"Yes. It's a position of honor and great standing to be a member of the Court."

"Which means they spend a lot of time here."

She looked at me, surprised. "But of course."

"Obviously." A bunch of people hanging around would become a problem later if I killed their king.

Not that I was planning on that. Not quite yet, at least.

We climbed higher and higher through the castle, using the broad, sweeping staircases that spiraled upward. The king lived at the very top, in a series of towers that were separated from the rest of the castle. The halls became less crowded as we neared, until eventually, I saw no one.

The woman stopped in front of an enormous silver door. A silver stag's head was inlaid into the broad surface, the horns protruding outward as if to warn people off.

Part of me wanted to turn around and run for it.

Not an option.

I drew in a steady breath.

My guide banged on the door, then announced our presence. "I've brought the winner of the trial."

The door swung open, but no one stood on the other side. The woman disappeared down the stairs, as quietly as smoke.

I strolled in, knowing that I should bow my shoulders and try to appear meek, but totally unable to do so. It might help my disguise, but I needed him to respect me.

Wanted him to, despite the fact that he was possibly a total asshole. A total murderous asshole.

The room itself was enormous—a circular tower with a high ceiling and many windows that let in the cool night breeze.

It was spartan, too, with just an enormous bed, dresser, and chair pulled up in front of a huge glass-less window.

He called me to his bedroom.

My heartbeat thundered, and I hoped his excellent hearing couldn't pick up on it.

Carefully, I kept my gaze away from the huge bed.

The king lounged in the chair in front of the window—which looked more like a throne—and gazed out at the city below. Fairy lights sparkled though the streets, lighting them as well as the street lamps we used on earth. As I understood it, they were an extension of Fae energy. Did the demon magic that was infecting this place have any effect on them?

I'd have to try to figure it out.

The king looked just as big in the chair as he did when he was standing. Just as lethal. There was no such thing as being caught off guard for this man, no matter how relaxed he looked. He was ready to spring at any moment.

He turned and gazed at me, green eyes bright in the dimly lit room. I keenly felt the lack of my usual armor. My hair, makeup, and dress were a disguise. But they were me all the same, and I was comfortable in them. This felt like going to a black-tie wedding in jeans and a T-shirt.

And then there was the issue with me being his *Mograh.*

Please let the spell work.

Suddenly, I felt like a butterfly. Wings pinned, helpless.

Even his gaze was strong. Devastating.

I straightened my spine and made sure that my voice sounded bored. "You rang?"

He smiled, and it was both cold and hot at the same time. When he rose, the movement was so graceful that it looked like he flowed to his feet without any effort at all. He was a good twenty feet away, but still, he seemed too tall.

It was the damned shoes. Without my heels, he towered even higher above me.

I hated how beautiful I found him. He was like the physically perfect form of masculinity, brought to life by a whisper of magic. I could just barely make out the points of his ears, and wondered how I'd missed them back at my place. Probably a glamour. Or his hair.

"Of course I called for you." His voice slipped over me like honey. "You've intrigued me. There's something about you that I just can't place."

"Oh?" I raised a brow, then strolled to another window in the room, desperate to put some space between us. It wasn't like my disguise was infallible. Getting too close was iffy. I stopped in front of the window and looked out at the sprawling Fae city beyond. "This place intrigues me."

"You've never been to a Fae realm?"

"No. Certainly not this one." There were several, but this was one of the most famous. Along with their opposite, the Unseelie realm, full of Dark Fae. They were the evil ones, according to the legend.

"No. Not many have been here. We keep our borders strictly guarded."

"Is that why you host the games? Because I have to say, as a tourist endeavor, it's a flop." I shook my head. "Too many people died. It looks bad."

He chuckled low in his throat, and the sound rubbed along my nerve endings in the best way. There was attraction and fear in equal measures...and I *liked* it.

Okay, weirdo.

"I will keep that in mind for the future," he said. "But tell me. Why did you save the wolf?"

"I already told you underneath the blackthorn tree."

He frowned, as if he didn't quite understand that I simply hadn't wanted to and that there was no ulterior motive. He'd expected me to have another answer, and I did not.

"And the lion shifter? You could have killed him."

"I didn't want to do that either."

"You saved the blue-haired Fae."

"Because I wanted to." I smiled and looked at him over my shoulder. "It all comes down to what I want."

"You played with honor. There are no points for honor."

He either didn't believe in honor or was trying to figure out if I did, and I couldn't decide which. "I got my points another way." I held up my hand, showing four fingers. "Four prizes, remember?"

"Yes, you're very skilled." He strolled toward me. "And somehow a bit familiar."

Ohhhh, shit. I turned to lean out the window,

pretending to try to get a better view but really just wanting to hide my face from him.

"Why do you host these deadly games?" I asked.

"We host the games because it is tradition. Because the prize at the end is so valuable that people are willing to die for it. So we let them."

"Hmm."

"And perhaps I like it."

"Do you really? Watching all those people die?"

"It's entertaining." His voice was aloof, but somehow I didn't quite buy it.

Which was probably just wishful thinking on my part, and that was dangerous. Becoming infatuated with the deadly, probably evil king was a *terrible* idea.

I felt Tarron stop behind me. He wasn't close enough that he was touching, but just like before, I could feel the heat of him.

It lit something up inside me as memories collided in my head. His lips on mine, his hands around my waist. The low groans he made as he kissed me.

It'd been the best kiss of my life.

And it'd been with a murderer.

He murdered his brother.

I wanted to ask him about that, but no way in hell that was happening.

"Why did you come here?" he asked.

"To win."

"What would you ask for if you won? What would your wish be?"

"That's my secret to keep." His nearness made me vibrate. It made heat race up my spine and shivers run back down. I swallowed hard and slipped away, headed for the bigger window. "You have an excellent view."

"You're avoiding me."

I looked over my shoulder at him and smiled. "Of course not."

He grinned, and it was a wolfish smile. "You are. But what if I happen to like stalking my prey?"

Oh, I had a feeling he did.

And also a feeling that I wouldn't mind *being* his prey.

I drew in a deep breath and focused on the task at hand. Was there anything in the room that might give me any clues?

The whole place was spartan. I'd expected a fancier lifestyle from a Fae king. But this one didn't seem to enjoy his rule. It wasn't just what Luna had said. Or this nearly empty room.

But him.

Maybe it was the knowledge I'd gained back in my workshop—that memory of his pain, whatever it was. He hid it well beneath an icy exterior.

There was something in the air, though. A darkness.

The demon magic, perhaps.

I stood at the window and looked out, silent.

There was probably nothing to be found in these barren rooms, and unless I could get him to drink a truth potion, I couldn't question him just yet. What I needed was a chance to sneak around and use my seeker sense. Maybe find the source of the darkness.

He appeared behind me.

I felt him more than heard him. I reached out to feel his magic to see if he felt like the darkness that was infecting his realm. Perhaps just a little. Or perhaps it was my imagination.

"Never heard of personal space, huh?" I asked.

"I'm the king. It's all my personal space."

I shivered, turned on and offended at the same time. Slowly, I drew in a steadying breath.

"Why do you hide from me?" he asked.

"Hide?"

"You drift from window to window."

"I've never seen the Fae realm. And maybe I don't want your attention, and I'm trying to be polite."

"That could be it. But you would at least look at me to show your displeasure. I've seen how you fight. You wouldn't mind fighting me, I would wager."

"You'd like that?"

"I think I would."

But shit, he was right. I wasn't playing my part right. I'd over-avoided. I needed to trust my guise. I turned to him, looking up.

Wow. He was tall.

And close.

The scent of him rolled over me. The forest, the wind. Something indescribably manly. My heart beat faster. "Why did you call me here?"

"For this." He gestured between us. "Just to see you. You are special, Mari."

It was strange to hear my name on his lips. Only Aeri ever used that name.

Now this man—this strange king with his dark and tortured past—was using it. And I liked it.

I *liked* it.

Dangerous.

When people show you who you are, believe them. It was my favorite Maya Angelou quote, and I lived my life by that. Attributing imaginary positive attributes to a man you were attracted to never ended well. This guy was showing me that he was callous with the lives of others—the contestants were just a game to him. He was a domineering king.

I should believe that and not fall prey to this attraction.

It was dangerous for women to think that they could fix a man who was broken. That it was worth it. Or even possible.

It wasn't.

Good men showed themselves to you for who they were—good.

This man had never done that, and my attraction was dangerous. Stupid.

But you saw inside his mind.

Didn't matter.

His nearness, though...

My mind and soul were swept up in it. I couldn't take it. His scent wrapped around me and his heat seeped into my bones. I nearly vibrated with the tension of standing so close to him.

It didn't matter that he was dangerous.

That's what I *liked.*

My breathing thickened, and heat raced over my skin. I couldn't help but look at his lips, full and soft. I wasn't keen on touching normally, but I *definitely* wanted to touch him.

From outside, the wind picked up. It blew my hair over my shoulder, and the midnight strands glowed with moonlight.

I gasped and stepped back, nearly going out the window.

"I need to go." Heart pounding, I slipped around him.

I could feel his gaze on me as I walked to the door. Tension prickled along my spine.

Nearly there. Nearly there.

Only ten feet from the door, and he hadn't called me back yet.

Magic sparked from behind me, sharp and bright.

I couldn't help it.

I turned.

The thorn wolf from the competition stood slightly behind the king, just to the left. Tarron turned to look at whatever had appeared.

He must have startled the one-eyed creature, who jumped and bit his hand as he turned.

The king cursed, jerking his hand away.

Fear flashed through me.

Don't hit the wolf.

The king just frowned down at the creature. In the millisecond that I watched, tension crackled on the air.

The king turned back to me. "Are you all right? You look like you've seen a ghost."

My gaze flashed up to his. "I thought you would hit the wolf."

It was exactly what a spoiled king would do. Even now, I could see blood dripping down his hand from the bite.

"I'll hit him later."

He was *joking*? I had to be sure. "No, you won't."

His gaze turned icy. "You don't know me."

He was right. These brief flashes of empathy from him —of simply not being an asshole—weren't enough.

"Is the wolf yours?" I asked, my gaze on the wolf.

"The thorn wolf goes where he pleases."

"Hmm." I turned to go.

"Mari."

I turned back.

The words seemed torn from him, as if he didn't want to say them but felt compelled. "I wouldn't hit the wolf. I startled him. It wasn't his fault that he reacted."

Shock raced through me. He didn't want me to think him evil.

What the hell did that mean?

I had no idea, so I just nodded. And left.

As I ran down the stairs from the king's chamber, I felt like

Cinderella fleeing the ball. Except I'd seen through his disguise, rather than the other way around.

No.

I was reading too much into the interaction with the wolf.

But how were they connected? Why had the wolf appeared?

It seemed like they were friends. No one could ever own the thorn wolf, but if the creature liked you, surely it would appear to you. And the king *had* been concerned about it.

I reached the landing at the base of the stairs that led to the king's tower. As with most of the castle, there were huge windows there. No glass, just a perfect endless view of the beautiful city and the river and mountains beyond. A breeze blew, cool and refreshing.

This place had to have great weather all the time if they never put glass in their windows.

I was both jealous of that and bored by the idea.

The sound of ladies laughing echoed from the hall to my left. My heart rate jumped, and I looked over. I couldn't see them, but they'd be turning the corner any moment.

Shit.

This was my chance. I'd managed to distract the king enough that he'd let me leave without a chaperone—I could probably thank the wolf for that—and now I had my opportunity.

I hurried down the next flight of stairs, then slipped into the first dark corner I could find. I crowded in behind a statue of an enormous stag—these Fae *really* loved their stags—and held my breath.

The ladies from above trooped down the stairs and continued onward, their flowing dresses trailing behind them in sweeps of jewel-toned silk.

The Court.

A Court with nothing to do, probably. He definitely didn't seem like your normal Seelie Fae, ready to make merry and party with his admirers.

This all had to do with the demon energy. It *had* to. Something was deeply wrong in this wonderland, and I needed to figure it out.

I closed my eyes and called upon my seeker sense. It was the weakest of my powers, but if I combined it with my amplification magic, I might get enough magical juice that I could find the source of this darkness. Because it had to be coming from somewhere.

I hadn't sensed it on the king—at least not in great enough quantities that I could consider him to be the source—so it had to be coming from somewhere else.

Power sparked deep in my soul. I focused on it, fanning it to life with my will.

Come on. Come on.

I imagined being able to find what I sought—the source of this dark magic that the Seelie Fae were too naive to even sense in their own realm. Because if they knew something was wrong, I got no sense of it. They hadn't even connected the deaths with it.

Though perhaps they were being enchanted? There could be something at work that kept them from noticing.

I drew in a deep breath and combined my amplification magic with my seeker sense. I envisioned them as red and yellow mists mixing together. Tricks like these often helped me manipulate my power.

Where is the source of this dark energy?

After a moment of sheer, terrifying nothing, I got a hint. There was a slight tug at my middle as my seeker sense ignited. It pulled me down and to the back of the castle.

It had to be there.

Once I was sure the coast was clear, I darted out from my hiding space. Silent as a thief, I slipped through the castle, going down stairs and across halls, my way illuminated by sparkling fairy light. In one room, there were tables laden with delicious foods. The fruit gleamed invitingly, and my stomach growled.

I'd eaten after the competition, but it called to me even so.

No.

I must not. There were stories about the Fae fruit. Eat the wrong one and you might stay forever.

Whatever ball or party these tables were for, they would remain untouched by me. I hurried past, resisting the urge to have a snack, and kept going through a room where diaphanous pale blue silk hung in front of the windows. It waved in the breeze, moonlight shining through it, and it was perhaps the most beautiful thing I'd ever seen.

This Seelie realm was a trip, all right.

I wished for Aerie. For her crotchety hellcat Wally. For my friends from Magic's Bend.

For anything that would remind me of my world at home and not this crazy one of Fae beauty and a reluctant king with a dark and terrifying past.

This place was messing with my head.

Finally, I reached the back of the castle. I slipped through a quiet side door and out into the fresh air. I sucked in a deep breath, then pressed myself against the wall, taking stock of my seeker sense.

It continued to pull me back toward the rear of the castle. The curtain wall that surrounded the massive structure was huge. There had to be acres and acres inside of this place. At the very rear, there was a forest.

The trees were big, but not huge. Only a hundred feet tall, as opposed to the three or four hundred feet of the trees that surrounded the castle compound.

Dark energy seemed to seep from them, a slimy, snaky mist that crept along the ground. Could the Fae really not see this?

Probably not, or they'd do something about it.

I was particularly good at sensing this kind of thing, after all. A natural born talent combined with my job as a demon slayer.

"Mari? What are you doing here?"

I nearly leapt out of my skin at the sound of the voice.

I turned to see Luna, the Fae from earlier. She stood to the left, partially behind me. She had a knack for showing up. In her hands, she held a jug and a bowl.

I sucked in a breath to calm my breathing. "Taking a walk. You?"

"Getting a snack."

My gaze darted to the trees. I pointed. "What is that place?"

"The King's Grove."

"Like, the king's trees?"

"Basically. No one is allowed to go there. It is for him alone."

Huh. And the dark magic was coming from there.

"Cool." I glanced at the ground near the trees in the distance. I could definitely see the dark mist of black magic. A similar substance to the grime that covered Darklane, though we had our evil shit under control.

She clearly didn't sense anything, and I didn't want her to see me go toward the grove.

"Headed back to our quarters?" I asked. "I'll walk with you."

I'd have to find a way to slip away before we entered, but I didn't want this to be the last place she saw me.

"I can go partway with you. But I want to get some more cereal."

"Great."

We walked together for a few minutes, discussing the competition earlier that day. When she veered off for the kitchen, I kept going. Once I was sure she wasn't looking, I looped back around and raced toward the grove.

When I reached it, I hurried on, heading toward the wood. When I stepped through the trees, it was darker inside. The repellent magic that prickled against my skin was likely the king's protection charm to keep his grove private.

Or it could be the demon magic I was hunting.

As I made it deeper into the woods, I spotted a sturdy stone wall built between the trees. They looked like oaks, and they grew up through the stone wall, entwined with the structure. It contained an area of unknown size, but it was totally blocked off.

As I neared the wall, my steps slowed. There was a gate, and beyond the gate, a roiling stench of dark magic that turned my stomach. Brimstone and putrid night lilies.

9

SLOWLY, I CREPT TOWARD THE GATE. MY SLIPPERS CRUNCHED on leaves, and a single sliver of moonlight shined through the canopy of leaves high above. The beam of light high-lighted the big metal lock.

I stopped in front of it, dark magic crawling across my skin. In addition to the smell that was so similar to my mother's, it felt like huge spiders and tasted like rotten eggs. I shuddered from the strength of it.

Shit. Oh, double shit.

I'd expected to find something tonight.

But maybe not this.

Whatever was beyond this gate...it was bad.

I raised a hand to the gate and touched the lock, a shiver racing up my arm. Magic sparked from the lock, a protective charm that would be hard to break.

For anyone but me.

I drew in a steady breath and sliced my thumb with my nail. Pain flared and blood welled.

Time to make some magic.

I called upon my Dragon Blood power, envisioning the gift of spell breaking. It was a rare and difficult magic, and it took a lot of energy to create. By the time I felt the power tingling at my fingertips, my breath was coming short and my muscles were weak.

I funneled more magic into the power, crafting it from nothing. This would be a valuable skill to have if I were willing to create it permanently.

But I wasn't. I couldn't risk it. Too much magic and my signature would change forever. Each new skill made it grow, and if I had too many skills, it'd be obvious to anyone what I was.

Not worth it.

Once I felt the power of the spell breaker flowing through my veins, I fed it into the lock. Black mist swirled around the complex metal structure, until finally, the sparking pain of the protective charm faded away. There was a pop in the air, and it was done.

Now that the repelling charm was gone, I could get to work on the lock. I drew two pins from my hair and knelt, sticking the little pieces of metal into the hole. It took a few minutes—the king had spared no expense on this sucker —but the lock finally clicked open.

I shoved the pins back into my hair and slipped through the gate, entering a forest that was so full of dark magic I nearly stumbled.

The walls had done a lot to contain it, which meant they were probably imbued with another spell.

I raised my skirt to my mouth and nose, breathing shallowly through the cloth to avoid the stink. Dread chilled my skin as I started through the forest. I drew my dagger from the ether and crept on silent feet, muscles tensed for whatever was ahead.

Oh fates, what would I find?

No way my mother would just be sitting in these woods, if she was even involved with this, but perhaps a clue?

When I stumbled on the clearing, I blinked in confusion.

A massive crystal obelisk jutted from the earth. The rock was roughly rectangular, but extremely thin and very tall. Around it, the ground was cracked and blackened.

The dark magic seemed to seep from it, curling over the ground like mist.

What the hell was it?

I'd expected something more than this.

But a rock?

Why a rock?

Standing stones were vitally important to the Fae. Was that what this was?

But there was only one, and it was so evil it felt like the devil himself had put it there.

My steps slowed as I approached, and the magic grew stronger. The stench was so powerful that I almost couldn't breathe, and the feeling of repulsive prickling became one of daggers stabbing me in the chest. Pain surged through me, and my eyes pricked with tears. My limbs grew heavy and reluctant to continue, but I forced myself onward.

How could I destroy this?

Because it *had* to be destroyed. This was what was polluting the Fae realm. And somehow it had caused the deaths of all those people.

I kept going, nearly there. Only twenty feet to go. But every step grew more difficult, every breath more painful.

No. I have to stop.

If I continued, I would die. The crystal obelisk would suck the life right from me. Worse, the desire to kill was starting to filter into my mind.

It was so strange and sudden that I nearly gasped. Or I would have, if I weren't nearly frozen solid by the dark magic that was twisting around me. Only now did I see the black mist. It had hovered around my feet, nearly invisible in the dark.

It crept up my legs, up my waist.

My heart thundered as horror swelled inside my chest.

No, no, no.

I tried to turn, to run. I clawed at my hair, trying to drive away the visions of me sacrificing people to this dark stone. Blood flowed through my mind, screams echoed.

I collapsed, no longer able to move. To think.

I was a creature of the crystal obelisk, fully victim to its whims. A tool.

Tears poured down my cheeks as consciousness began to fade.

Something clamped around my ankle. Pain flared briefly, panic following. Something had bitten me. It dragged me through the forest, away from the stone. Fear made me want to fight, but I was too weak.

By the time the creature dragged me through the gate, the worst of the mind-fogging evil had faded from my head. I gasped, sitting upright, muscles aching and breaths heaving. My limbs were weak and my head fuzzy.

The thorn wolf sat in front of me, his one good eye glued to me.

"You saved me."

The wolf just looked at me. Then he disappeared.

"Holy fates." I drew a shaking hand over my sweaty brow, then turned to the gate.

It was still open.

I staggered upright and stumbled toward it, then shut it as quickly as I could. It took longer to re-lock it without the key. My hairpins kept shaking in my trembling hands.

Finally, it clicked back into place. I leaned my head against the gate, panting. That would have to be good enough. I couldn't redo the charm. But I'd have to find a way to destroy that stone before it destroyed this place.

I just had no idea how.

The next morning came early. It was probably my exhaustion from the night before, along with the dreams that had haunted me, but I was still aching the next day. When the hobgoblin woke me with a clanging bell and a tray of food, I wanted to cry.

Instead, I ate.

I would need my strength. If I could keep going in this competition, I could win the prize and wish for the evil crystal obelisk to be destroyed. Though I'd wanted the prize for my own, to figure out what my other bloodline really was, I couldn't use it that way now.

Because whatever the stone really was, it needed to be destroyed. By any means possible. That evil couldn't be allowed to take over the Fae realm and then earth. If my mother was involved in this, I might figure out her identity anyway.

And the king needed to be dealt with. He'd locked it up —to protect it, or to protect others from it?

Impossible to say. But I didn't want to question him until I knew more. If he were actually evil, he could throw me right out of the kingdom or, more likely, into a Fae dungeon.

I finished my breakfast and turned my mind to the competition ahead. Fortunately, my clean clothes had been delivered, and I dressed quickly. Again, I felt naked without my makeup and hair, but it was my best disguise here. I'd already updated Aeri last night about what I'd found, and she would be telling the Council of Demon Slayers. They'd arrange backup if I determined that I needed it.

For now, my only job was to try to beat the other

competitors and win this damned prize. On the way, I'd figure out what the king's role was.

As with yesterday, we met in the arena. Though it was morning, the stands were full and the crowd cheering. Tarron stood in his usual box, staring down at me.

Did he know what I'd done last night?

No. He couldn't.

The Fae announcer landed in front of the four of us. Today, her dress was a molten gold that matched her hair, which had changed color overnight. She swept out her arms, her voice booming. "Contestants! Welcome! You are here to compete in the second round. The most exciting round. It will be longer, and more difficult, but at the end, one of you will reach the prize—the coveted Wish Stone that will grant you one thing you truly desire."

The crowd cheered, roaring.

The announcer continued. "Today you will be returning to the earthly realm. To the sacred glen of Kilmartin. This area, enormous in size, is the home of more ancient, sacred Fae monuments than anywhere in the world. It is the gateway to our realm, and here, you will continue to compete amongst the shadows of history."

Okay, that was cool but all very vague.

"Each of you will begin a treasure hunt, full of riddles and mysteries that you must solve to reach the final prize. There are particular parts of this journey that are the most entertaining. There, magic will project your image into this arena so that the spectators may watch you. When that happens, you will feel it. Now, it is time to depart!" With a flourish of her hands, four beautiful carriages appeared. Each was pulled by a pair of winged stags.

We each climbed into a carriage under the expectant gaze of the crowed. The stags took off, cantering through the arena. The crowd cheered and screamed, and I couldn't help but smile.

I didn't hate being adored.

I was going to assume that's what the cheers were about.

When the stags reached the edge of the arena, they took off into the air, their powerful wings carrying us high. I gasped and gripped the side of my carriage. The wind tore at my hair and the sun shined brightly as we traveled over the city.

It sprawled out below us, beautiful and pristine. I couldn't see the King's Grove because the obelisk was shielded by the trees.

By the time we reached the portal to the human realm, I was windblown and ready to get on with the challenge. The stags trotted right through the portal and into the other side.

When they appeared in Kilmartin, their wings disappeared. The glow that surrounded their bodies faded as well. It was as if earth was dampening their magic. This was the border between the Fae world and the human one, but it was still earth.

The carriages split up at that point, the stags taking us each in different directions. I watched the carriage carrying Luna disappear to the east, toward the rising sun, while the lion went west.

Before mine could move, I leaned forward. "Wait here a minute, will you?"

The two stags stopped, quivering. The Fae announcer had said that I'd feel it if I were being watched. I couldn't feel anything.

Probably safe.

I hopped down, then sprinted to the spot where I'd hidden my iron knife. This was the perfect time to have it. I was on earth, so I wasn't breaking their rules, but I'd potentially be going up against Fae challenges, so it could come in handy.

I recovered the dagger and returned to the carriages. The stags took me south. By the time the carriage stopped, the morning sun had burned the dew off the grass. The two stags looked expectantly back at me.

"Fine, fine. I'm getting out." I climbed from the carriage, and the stags took off, trotting into the distance.

I spun in a circle, taking in Kilmartin Glen. It was flat and green and beautiful, with mountains on two sides and the water far in the distance at one end. There were tiny specs of gray along the landscape—probably the ancient stone monuments that the announcer had mentioned.

But where to next?

I turned one more circle, calling upon my seeker sense. It tugged me west, and I turned, finally spotting the thorn wolf about half a mile in the distance.

I frowned.

Why was this guy always turning up?

He'd been with the king last night...

Was he his emissary? Could the king perhaps see through his eye?

Nah. The wolf seemed like his own creature.

He was standing in the direction I needed to go, though. Was he leading me?

He'd chosen to help me last night. And in the arena the day before, when he'd kept my horrible memories at bay while I'd climbed the pillar.

I headed for the wolf, following my seeker sense and intuition. I had no idea if it was cheating that he was trying to help, but he was partially the king's animal, so it had to be okay.

And honestly, I didn't care about winning fairly. I just needed to win.

When I reached the wolf, I realized that he stood in front of a huge expanse of flat rock that protruded from the grass. It was dark from the last of the morning mist, but I was able to make out carved spots on the rock.

I knelt to inspect them, noticing that most of them were circles with rings carved around them. A bit like Saturn.

I looked up at the wolf, feeling like someone was watching me.

But the wolf was staring off into the distance, his gaze nowhere near me.

No, of course not.

I was probably being watched by the audience. I shivered, uncomfortable. It sucked.

I stood and spun in a circle, looking for some kind of recording device. It'd definitely be magic, but I saw nothing. All the same, I had a feeling they were watching, somehow.

Annoyed, I turned back to the stone, my gaze traveling over the many carved inscriptions.

I glanced at the wolf. "What do you think it is?"

He looked at me with his one good eye. *Bacon.*

I laughed and frowned at him. "Did you just speak in my mind?"

Bacon.

"Is that the only word you know?"

Bacon.

I laughed again. It was freaking hilarious that this noble beast who provided aid when I needed it also said, "Bacon."

"I'll get you bacon when this is done, all right? To thank you for the help."

The wolf inclined his head.

Okay, then. I owed the thorn wolf some bacon.

Until then, I needed to figure out what these symbols were. I stared at them for a moment longer, then inspected the terrain around me. In the distance, I could see a hill fort, a stone circle, a pile of rocks. There were more gray dots in the distance—more monuments—but those were the big three. And when I stood on this side of the big flat rock in front of me, it looked like the inscriptions on the stone lined up with the main three monuments.

"Is it a map?" I asked.

Bacon.

"Does that mean yes?"

Bacon.

"Yeah, it means yes, I'm going to guess." I pointed at the map, where one long line had been carved. "If my theory is right, that is the waterline that we see over there, where the sea is."

The wolf just looked at me. He didn't even say bacon. But I felt good about this theory.

I knelt at the edge of the stone again, noticing that one of the carvings was glowing slightly. I looked up at the landscape, my gaze landing on the pile of rocks in the distance.

"The glowing bit corresponds with the pile of rocks," I said to the thorn wolf.

Silence.

"I'm going to take that as a yes." I stood, then started for the rocks. They had to be a good two miles away.

"Thank you for the help." I looked at the thorn wolf. "What is your name?"

Bacon.

"Your name is bacon?"

Bacon.

That was neither a yes nor a no, so I'd have to decide later if he was named Bacon. Seemed unlikely.

"Well, thank you."

The thorn wolf nodded.

I called upon my magic, transporting to the pile of rocks in an instant. The wolf didn't follow, though I wished he had. I quite liked a sidekick.

Carefully, I focused on the atmosphere. I could just barely get a sense of being watched. I could just imagine myself being displayed in the middle of the arena.

"So what are you?" I murmured to the pile of rocks as I walked in a circle around it. The pile itself was about sixty feet across and ten feet high. There were thousands of head-sized rocks piled on top of each other. It looked like a mess, frankly.

Then I reached the far edge.

There was an entrance.

Three huge slabs of rock had been used to create the frame of a door. The door itself was made of another slab of rock, wedged perfectly in place.

It had to be a chambered cairn. My friend Cass had told me all about them, though I'd never seen one myself.

I stepped back, studying it.

Clearly, I had to get in.

I approached the door, which had no hinges. Just two carved divots that might be handholds, placed right at the top. Reverently, I placed my palms on the stone, focusing on the feel of it beneath my hands.

I could sense no repelling magic. It was actually almost inviting.

I stepped back and inspected the ground. There was a

small trench in the earth beneath the door, right in front. With the handholds at the top...

An idea occurred. Maybe it was simple. I'd just pull on it like a drawbridge going down.

I placed my hands in the two divots and pulled down. The stone creaked and groaned. I gave it a bit more effort, grateful for my enhanced strength.

As I pulled, the bottom of the door fit perfectly into the little trench. It'd been carved there so the door would pull open relatively easily.

I kept pulling, sweat dripping down my brow as I worked. This was definitely a multi-person job, but I kept at it. Finally, the stone door fell perfectly into place.

Cold air rushed out of the dark tunnel in front of me. Not a single bit of light emitted from within, but slowly my eyes adjusted. The sun provided just enough of a glow, and I stepped in.

Something in front of me made me stop abruptly.

A little clay jar.

Should I pick it up?

I hovered my hand over it, feeling a slight pulse of magic. But also of reverence.

No. I probably shouldn't pick it up. I withdrew my hand. There were other things in the tunnel as well. A bone comb, and a flute. Four more jars. I touched nothing. Somehow, it seemed important that I touch nothing.

Each time I came across another artifact, I carefully stepped around it. When I reached the end of the tunnel, I stopped.

Magic sparked from the ground, and I bent to touch it.

A moment later, I stood in the middle of a field.

I jerked upright. "What the hell?"

The end of the tunnel within the chambered cairn had been a portal.

Of course.

I could no longer feel the tingle of the magic that indicated that the audience was watching. It was just me.

I spun in a circle. The land around me wasn't much different from the one I'd just left. The terrain looked much the same, with flat green plains bordered by mountains. A blue sky full of fluffy clouds and the sea sparkling in the distance.

There were no stone monuments, but there was a grove of trees to my right. I used my seeker sense, commanding it to find me answers.

It tugged me toward the grove. It was close enough that I didn't bother teleporting—I should save my power, anyway. It was finite, and I didn't know when I'd get to rest and recoup.

Fairy lights sparkled around the tops of the trees, and birds called from the branches.

Tension thrummed along my veins as I approached the trees. At the edge, I drew in a deep breath, then stepped into the grove.

10

I STEPPED THROUGH THE TREES INTO A CLEARING. A WOMAN sat in the middle of the space, her gown as green as the grass that surrounded her. The copper of her hair glinted in the sun, and she looked up at me.

Her blue eyes met mine, and I felt like she could see right into my soul. Slowly, I approached. As I neared, I realized that it was impossible to determine her age. She was inconceivably beautiful, but ageless.

All around, animals moved between the trees. Rabbits, foxes, a badger. They seemed at harmony here, not afraid of anything—even though the foxes would normally eat the rabbits.

Frankly, it was eerie.

I stopped in front of the woman, who gestured for me to sit.

I did as she requested, mimicking her cross-legged position.

"Are you a seer?" I asked.

She had to be. Her energy was so distinct. Sitting in her presence felt like sitting at the juncture between the past and present and future.

"I am indeed. The Iona."

I searched my mind. Why would this competition put me on the path to find a seer? "Can I ask you how to find the final prize at the end of this journey?"

There were more things I wanted to ask, but I needed to find out the parameters first.

"Yes, that is a question I can answer." She waved her hand in front of her, and a stone bowl appeared. A pestle appeared next. She looked up and met my gaze. "To answer this question for you, I must have something of yours."

I reached up and pulled out a long black hair, then handed it over. "Will that do?"

"It will." She placed it in the bowl, then waved her hand over the grass next to her.

A collection of items appeared. A cluster of berries, two little rocks, a bowl of water, and a pile of dirt that rose up from the grass below.

She picked up the berries and dropped them into her stone bowl. "Rowan berries for life." She added the rocks. "For strength." The dirt. "For balance." Last, she poured the water into the bowl. "For direction."

She picked up the pestle and ground the rocks and dirt into the berries and water, then waved her hand over the mixture. Her palm glowed bright white, and the light filtered down into the bowl.

The Fae were very into nature magic, and this definitely fit the bill. As her light glowed into the bowl, the bright sun around us faded to dark.

I shivered.

The Fae seer removed her hand with a flourish, and a burst of white mist exploded up from the bowl. It traveled toward the sky, filling it with night stars.

The Fae dropped to her back and stared at the sky.

I watched her, a bit confused, then mimicked her movement. I might as well look at the stars too. Maybe they'd tell me something.

Except when I stared at them, they just looked like normal stars. The Fae seer muttered under her breath, and it had the cadence of a spell. Magic sparked along the air and my skin, then I felt her sit up.

I joined her, meeting her gaze. It was vacant and strange, and when she spoke, her voice was deep with power. "You are on a path to defeat the darkness."

Shock lanced me. "The darkness in the Fae realm?"

"You must not fail."

"What about the king? Does he know about the darkness in his realm? Did he bring it here?"

She ignored my questions, the words flowing from her lips as if forced. "To get to the prize, you will need a key. It is drowned in the darkness with the Unseelie Mer."

"What does that mean?"

She kept talking, her words rolling over mine. "It will open the gate to the Rowan Grove."

"What gate?"

"It can be found at the ring where the sun will reset the world on the highest day of summer."

Oh boy, talk about esoteric. "Can you explain more about—"

The ether sucked me in, the portal returning me to the darkness of the chambered cairn.

I gasped, grabbing the stone wall next to me for support.

Holy fates.

My head spun as I adjusted. Clearly the Fae seer was done with me. But what the hell had that all meant?

I had no freaking idea.

I bent toward the ground again, trying to trigger the portal to take me back to her.

It didn't work.

I tried again.

Nothing.

Shit.

I drew in a steady breath. She'd been talking about Fae stuff. Their myths and lore were tied up with this entire task.

Think. Think. I could do this.

But not in here. It was too dark and close, and I was pretty sure that the clay jugs on the ground were full of the ashes of dead people.

Carefully, I picked my way out through the tunnel, arriving in the bright light of day.

I blinked, temporarily blind in the sun. When my

vision cleared, I spotted Tarron. The king stood near the exit, leaning against a tree I hadn't noticed before. Had he made it grow there?

He no longer wore the suit from yesterday. Instead, he was dressed in clothes more suited to the kind of danger I'd be facing out here. Leather boots, sturdy pants of a deep midnight blue, and thin green sweater with a brown leather jacket. Had to be modern Fae fight wear.

"What are you doing here?" I demanded as I approached.

"Did you learn anything good?"

"Answer my question."

"I'm interested in you."

"Cut straight to the punch, don't you?"

"I'm the king. Of course I do. There's no point in dancing around."

"Yeah, you're the king. Which means you probably shouldn't be here. Aren't we being watched by the audience?" I couldn't feel the prickle of awareness that meant we were being watched, but I'd felt it before I'd walked into the cairn.

He waved a hand, clearly unconcerned. "I've created a bit of magical static. I'd prefer they not see me here."

"I don't understand why you're so interested. None of this makes sense." Dare I mention the crystal obelisk I'd found in his grove last night?

No. Not yet. I didn't know if I could trust him.

"I wouldn't worry about it," he said. "You're beautiful. That's enough reason for me to be interested."

He moved, skillfully managing to get me with my back to the tree. I gasped, trying to hide my reaction. He loomed over me, tall and broad. Sunlight glinted off his hair.

"What are you doing?" My breath came short.

"I've no idea what you mean." He crowded me closer to the tree, his scent wrapping around me.

Tension thickened between us, an awareness that made my heart thunder. My gaze moved to his lips, and memories of kissing him flashed through my mind.

I want to kiss him.

I ducked out and to the right.

I didn't have time for this.

Was he here to distract me so I wouldn't win? "I need to get a move on."

"Perhaps I can help you."

"Really? Is that even in the rules?"

"I'm the king."

Uncertain, I chewed on my lip and studied him. He was here, interested in me. Whatever his reasons—and I didn't buy that it was solely because he was attracted to me —did they really matter?

"Do you want me to win this?"

He shrugged. "Not particularly concerned on that front, no."

"Then why would you help me?"

"Entertainment?"

Did I believe that? Not really. There was something else at play here.

But he was Fae, and I could use the help. He might be

able to help me with the riddle from the seer. "Something is going to happen early tomorrow morning. It's the summer solstice, correct? That's the highest day of summer."

"Correct."

Good. I could already guess that the ring where the sun would reset the world in the morning was a stone circle. They were often built to align with solstices. It was very logical, in their magical Fae way. It would have to be the biggest one in the region. But the Unseelie Mer...

"The seer said that I will need a key to access the gate, and it can be found 'drowned in the darkness with the Unseelie Mer.' What the hell are the Unseelie Mer?"

"She must mean the Finfolk. Like the Merfolk. But dark. Often evil, like the Unseelie." Disgust echoed in his voice.

He really didn't like the Unseelie. "They are an Unseelie version of Merfolk? Dark to your light, like the Unseelie and the Seelie?"

"Exactly. But where is all of this supposed to take you? Where does the gate lead?"

"To the Rowan Grove." I watched him closely for any sign of surprise or interest. "Accessed by an ancient stone circle."

How much did he know about what was to come? Was he possibly trying to get information out of me? Maybe I should play it closer to the vest and stick to getting information rather than giving it.

I turned from him, inspecting the terrain around me. "So I need to find the Unseelie Mer. The Finfolk."

Tarron strode up to stand beside me and pointed to the coastline. "They live in the ocean."

"Thanks."

"Anytime." With that, he disappeared.

Weird.

I called upon my transport magic and let the ether suck me in and take me to the coast. The sea air whipped my hair back from my face, and I stood on the rocks, looking out across the choppy waves. Sunlight glittered on the waves, making it difficult to see beneath the water.

How the heck did I find the Unseelie Mer here? And here was a whole ocean to search.

I knelt at the water and stuck my hand in, calling upon my seeker sense. I tried to find any hint of a prize, or even the Unseelie Mer themselves, but nothing came to me.

A moment later, a head popped up through the surface.

A beautiful girl blinked at me. "What are you doing?"

I stood and frowned. Her golden hair wafted in the water, and her skin was tinged slightly green. Slits at her neck indicated gills. "Are you an Unseelie Mer?"

She gasped, clearly offended. "I am *not.*"

"I'm sorry." I held up my hands. "Apologies."

"Those sorry excuses for Merfolk live in the dark lake farther inland. We drove them from the ocean generations ago, after they levied an attack against our people."

"Wait, what? They don't live in the ocean."

She scoffed. "Of course not."

The king had lied to me. Or he hadn't known.

I'd put my money on lie.

The bastard.

Why?

"Are you looking for the Unseelie Mer?" Her brow wrinkled.

"Not precisely." I explained the riddle to her that the seer had told me.

"Well, I don't know anything about that, but I can give you some advice if you like."

"Okay?"

"Payment first."

"What do you want?"

"What do you have?" Her eyes glittered keenly.

"Weapons. Potions."

"Ohhhh, I'm quite keen on the sparkly bits."

"Well, let's see, then." I drew my shiniest silver dagger from the ether. It was inset with a bright red gem.

She grinned widely. "I like that."

"It's yours for info about the Unseelie Mer."

"You'll need to be careful. Do not go in the water."

"Why not?"

"It would be a declaration of war for any Fae to enter the realm of the Unseelie Mer."

"I'm not Fae."

She tilted her head to the side. "You're not?"

"No."

"Hmmm. Then I suppose you won't be declaring war.

But do not look directly into their eyes, or they will enchant you into becoming their wife."

"A literal fishwife?"

She laughed, then scowled. "Don't joke. They are dangerous. If you make eye contact, they will drag you down and you will become bride of the deep."

Yeah, no thanks. Not for me. "I appreciate the info. Do you know how I would find their lake?"

She pointed to something behind me. "Go stand on that hill, then you will see it."

"Thank you." I trusted her. More than the king, at least. I handed her the blade.

She admired it briefly, then looked up. "Remember. No eye contact."

"Got it."

She waved, then popped back under the water.

I transported to the hill she'd pointed to, and almost immediately, my gaze caught on a patch of dark water in the distance. It was a huge lake, the top shining black and bright in the sunlight.

"That's got to be it." I ran down the hill, racing for the pond. Wind began to blow, fierce and strong. My hair whipped in the wind and my eyes stung from the howling gale. I bent low against it and plowed on.

There was no rain—not even any clouds—but the wind was fierce.

Where the hell had it come from?

I squinted my eyes nearly closed and kept on plowing forward, barely able to move as the wind shrieked by me.

What the hell was this?

I squinted left and right to see if the trees in the distance were shaking. They weren't—it was only blowing on me.

I caught sight of a figure far in the distance, tall and strong. He had jet black hair, and his strong arms crossed over his chest as he watched.

Tarron.

He was Fae. He could control the elements, wind included.

Was this bastard doing this to me?

Son of a bitch.

No more running for me.

I called upon my magic, letting the ether suck me in and drag me through space. A moment later, I appeared at the edge of the lake. The dark water wasn't black, as I'd expected, but rather a clear dark blue.

I turned to look for Tarron. He'd disappeared. I shook my head, irritation flickering inside me.

Carefully, I inspected the pond. There was a key here, but it might not appear as a key. I walked around the perimeter, searching intently. A moment later, I spotted a glow deep in the water. Important things glowed in this competition.

I toed off my boots and began to shuck off my clothes. I could feel the prickle of magi that meant the spectators were watching. Well, I was going to give them an eyeful, because I didn't want to run around in wet stuff this whole time. I left only my bra and panties. Then I waded into the lake, shivering at the cold.

There was no way this was going to be a nice, easy swim. I'd never really liked the water either.

I charged in anyway, ready to get it over with. When I was up to my waist, I sucked in a deep breath and dived deep. Cold water closed over my head, and I opened my eyes to see an emerald green world. Weeds waved in the beams of sunlight, and silver fish darted.

I kicked deeper, headed toward the golden glow at the bottom. The weeds slipped by my skin as I swam. Fear pierced me at the idea that they might wrap around me, but they just waved peacefully in the water.

I was nearly to the golden object when a figure flashed by to the right. Out of the corner of my eye, I could just barely make out that it was roughly human shaped, though it did have a fin. Scales covered the rest of its body, along with a fringe of spines along the back.

I diverted my eyes, keeping them glued on the object. Water pressure distorted my vision, so it was impossible to see exactly what it was.

My lungs burned as I went deeper. The figure flashed by to the left again. Closer this time. My heart thundered into my lungs. The thing brushed against my side, and I nearly screamed.

I called on a dagger from the ether and gripped it in my hand as I swam deeper. It was the iron blade, the one that I'd hidden and retrieved. The Finfolk were a type of Fae, and I was here to win.

When the hand grabbed my arm, horror shot through my chest. I did *not* like the water, and this wasn't helping. I lashed toward the hand, stabbing down with my blade. It plunged into the arm, and the creature hissed loudly, yanking its limb back.

Through squinted eyes, I barely caught sight of a broad face and distinct gills. There was a flash of yellow eyes, but I squeezed mine shut immediately.

Don't make eye contact.

I waved the blade in front of me, a threat of iron, then spun back toward the key and kicked for it. I opened my eyes just enough to see the golden glow and make sure I was on track.

Finally, I reached it and grabbed the tiny golden disk. I couldn't swim with my dagger and the disk gripped in both hands, so I shoved the disk in my sports bra, which was big enough and tight enough to contain the little object.

With the key safely in place, I turned to swim back to the surface.

And came face-to-face with a waiting Unseelie Mer.

The creature's yellow eyes caught mine, and I stared, unable to look away. I could feel the hilt of my dagger in my hand, but couldn't make myself use it.

The creature reached for me with a rough green hand and grabbed my arm, pulling me deeper into the water. His touch snapped me back to attention, and I struggled, trying to break free. But my movements were too weak, as if part of me wanted to go with him. My body fought my mind.

No!

I screamed, bubbles escaping my mouth. It took everything I had to curl myself forward and slash my blade at his scaled green torso, but I was too slow. He was an acrobat in the water, and now that he knew I held iron, he was fast.

My blade swiped through a weed, missing the creature entirely. My lungs burned with pain I'd never felt before. I thrashed and struggled, but couldn't break free.

There was a flash of movement in front of me. A person.

Tarron.

He kicked toward the Unseelie Mer, breaking the creature's grasp on me. The king grabbed my arm and kicked toward the surface. I helped, using the last of my energy. My head broke through to the air and I gasped.

"Come on!" The king's grip tightened on my arm, and he dragged me to shore. I kicked from behind him, weak and exhausted. I couldn't feel the prickle of magic that indicated that the spectators were watching, which meant he'd blocked their vision.

I crawled onto the shore, gripping my blade tight. The king bent down and swept me into his arms. His horns were out, sweeping back along the side of his head, and his eyes were a deep jet black. Fangs flashed in his mouth. The iron of my blade brushed his skin, and he hissed, jerking harshly.

"Steel?" His angry eyes met mine.

"I didn't bring it to your realm." I coughed, my lungs

burning.

Tarron's grip was warm and strong, tethering me to consciousness as I dragged in unsteady breaths.

"Then how did you get it? It is forbidden!"

"I hid it outside of the entrance to your realm. When the carriage passed by, I collected it. I guess no one was watching." I frowned at him. "And I'm glad I had it. It stopped the Unseelie Mer."

"The first time, maybe. Then I had to come and get you."

Finally, it dawned on me. "You...did. Why? You tried to stop me from getting here, but then you saved me."

"You were going to die. I couldn't let you."

He looked almost confused when he said it, and he sounded agonized. He'd been compelled to save me.

Because I was his *Mograh*.

Which he didn't realize because of the spell I'd done.

He was going to be *pissed* when he figured it out.

I met his gaze. "But isn't that an act of aggression against the Unseelie Mer for you to enter their waters?"

He set me on the ground, farther up from the water's edge. Gently, he gripped my shoulders to make sure that I was standing steady. "We'll see."

My gaze moved to the space beyond him. Three heads had appeared on the surface, each greener and uglier than the last. Fins surrounded their skulls like hair, and gills decorated their necks.

I looked away from the yellow eyes. "Look behind you."

The king turned. "Damn it."

11

TARRON STALKED TOWARD THE FINFOLK. HIS HORNS disappeared as he neared them, and I had a feeling that was an attempt at diplomacy.

Still shaking, I scrambled into my clothes. Before I zipped up, I confirmed that the golden charm was still wedged in my bra. I left it there, since it was the safest place, then stole glances at Tarron and the Finfolk.

They'd climbed out of the water onto sturdy legs. Their fins must have shifted, because I swore they'd had mermaid tails before.

Their posture was aggressive, but so was Tarron's. He'd only been willing to go so far with the diplomacy, it seemed.

He risked death to save me.

But then, he'd also tried to stop me from continuing in the competition. Between the howling gale and the lies, he'd actively tried to keep me from going any farther and getting the key.

He could have just let me die, and that would have finished the job nicely. But he hadn't been able to.

They spoke for five minutes, and each one crawled by. Finally, Tarron disappeared. The FinFolk gave me one last look, then returned to the water.

Well, shit.

That was that.

I turned and looked for a stone circle. It was nowhere to be seen.

There had to be multiple circles in an area so rich with history, but I'd definitely be looking for the biggest.

I called upon my seeker sense. As usual, it was weak. A bit of amplifying power made it stronger, but even then, I only got the slightest hint that I should go west. I looked up at the sky. My cell phone battery was dead after a full day in the Fae realm without power outlets, so I'd have to use the sun to measure time.

It was late afternoon, which meant there were at least twelve hours yet before sunrise. Given how big the glen of Kilmartin was and the fact that I was standing roughly in the middle, it was probably better to save my magic and walk. At least until I caught sight of the circle and could transport directly there instead of wasting my magic popping in and out of the ether to look for it. I'd already used it plenty.

Toward the west, I spotted a steep hill. It was only a mile away, at most.

I strode across the field. As I walked, the thorn wolf appeared at my side, strolling along.

"Hey, guy."

He woofed a greeting and trotted at my side.

I reached the steep hill, which seemed to jut out of the earth like a huge rocky castle. I began to climb, weaving my way past pink and blue flowers. I passed ancient broken walls and a deep hole that had probably been a well.

This had to be a hill fort with the castle long destroyed.

Wind tore at my hair when I reached the top, so strong that it nearly bowled me over. I tucked myself deeper into my short leather jacket and tried to ignore the chill.

From up there, I could see the entire glen. Almost immediately, my gaze landed on a huge stone circle, right next to a thick patch of trees.

"There it is." I pointed.

The wolf rumbled low in his throat, agreeing.

I looked down at him. "What should I call you?"

He just stared at me.

"Bruce?"

He shook his head.

"Pete?"

He shook again.

A word popped into my head. *Burnthistle.* "Is your name Burnthistle?"

His tongue lolled out in a smile.

"That's a mouthful. But okay, Burnthistle is cool. "Strange but cool. You do you, doggo."

He woofed.

"But it really is a mouthful. Would you want to be Burn for short?"

He woofed again.

"Let's call that a yes."

His tongue lolled out in a smile.

"Let's get moving, then." I climbed back down the hill and jumped over the broken walls to take a shortcut.

It didn't take long to reach the stone circle, which was constructed of thirteen towering stones that were decorated with the same pockmarks and concentric circles that I'd seen earlier on the flat stone that Burn had led me to. The diameter of the circle was probably about thirty feet across, and in the middle stood the tallest stone of all.

I hesitated at the outside of the ring. Magic sparked from within, both welcoming and repellent. It was the strangest combination, like hot and cold.

Burn disappeared, going wherever it was that he went.

"Now or never." I approached the circle.

There were still hours left—a whole night—before it would open. But I had to figure out where to put the key.

As I neared, I got the sense of being watched. That same feeling as before—when the audience was observing.

A breeze tousled my hair and hit my nose. I sniffed.

The faint animal smell of a shifter.

A *lion* shifter.

I whirled around.

The golden-haired lion shifter who'd bitten me

yesterday was prowling out from behind one of the stones. He was in his human form, tall and broad, with a mean tint to his golden eyes.

"I've been waiting for you," he growled.

"Yeah? Can't say I'm pleased to see you."

"You don't have to make this difficult."

I smiled. "But that's my specialty."

"Just give me your key and go on your way. I'll let you live."

"Ha. If you recall, I came out on top last time."

"Not this time." His magic surged around him as he pushed his signature out toward me. A threat.

"What happened to your key? Lose it?" He didn't answer, but the sullen expression on his face was enough to indicate that he probably had. "So, what? You've just been waiting here to ambush me?"

He shrugged. "Or the others. But you're my favorite." He smacked his lips. "You taste good."

His words reminded me of the morning that Tarron had tasted my blood and learned what I was. A shiver of unease passed over me. At least this guy hadn't seemed to notice that my blood was black and weird.

I drew my bow and arrow from the ether. "If you charge, I'm going to make this quick. I don't have time for an injury."

He just grinned as golden magic swirled around him. In the space of a heartbeat, he'd shifted into his lion form. His huge body glinted golden in the sun, and I had to remind myself that it was a man I was shooting, not a lion.

I had no problem shooting assholes, whereas I had no interest in shooting furry, fangy creatures. In fact, I was very fond of furry, fangy creatures.

The lion shifter raced toward me on powerful legs, mane blowing in the wind. He was so fast that my heart jumped.

I raised my bow and fired right at each of his legs. One arrow hit his front right leg, and he stumbled. The second arrow hit his other front leg, and he staggered.

He was nearly to me, so close that I could see the individual hairs of his mane. I fired the third, and he went down, skidding hard on the ground. I leapt out of the way, rolling to the side.

He pulled a burst of energy from somewhere and shoved himself off the ground, lunging after me. He was uncoordinated from the wounds, but managed to plow his body into mine. Pain flared in my ribs, sharp and bright.

His weight shoved me to the ground, and I kicked up, heaving him off of me. The force of my blow rolled him to the side, and I darted up, scrambling for my bow. As he struggled to his feet, I grabbed my bow and a fresh arrow and sent the projectile flying into his leg.

He roared and went down, all four limbs compromised. I lunged for him and slammed my bow down onto his head so hard that I heard the crack. He slumped unconscious.

I knelt over, inspecting where I'd hit him. Not bleeding. He'd wake up. Shifters were tough.

I stood and spun in a circle, shouting to the sky. "He's out! Come and get him."

I didn't know if the contest organizers could hear me, but I really wasn't in the mood to stand guard over the lion in case he woke up and I had to knock him out again. "I could kill him, but I won't. So come and get him. He doesn't stand a chance."

The air shimmered to my right, and four Fae appeared. They were each dressed in the pale blue and silver uniforms that seemed to be the official outfits of the palace guards who were working the competition. They approached at a swift pace.

I stepped back and waited as they took the shifter away. It didn't take them long to bundle him up and get him out of there. One of them approached me and handed me a pack.

"For tonight," the tall guard said.

I took it, and he left. As he walked away, I peeked inside the pack. A sleeping roll and a light dinner of bread, cheese, and fruit.

Yep. Looked like I'd be spending the night here.

Once I had the place to myself again, I inspected every stone carefully. It wasn't until I climbed to the top of the center stone, my ribs aching from the lion's blow, that I saw the tiny flattened area right in the middle. The perfect size for my little golden charm.

I pulled it out of my bra and put it in place, where it fit perfectly.

I grinned, then retrieved the stone and hopped down,

wincing slightly at the pain in my ribs. When it was closer to dawn, I'd put it back in place.

I returned to the shadows of the grove, which seemed like a good place to wait out the night. It gave me a view of the stone circle and a bit of protection from the elements.

I sat against a tree and ate my dinner as the sun set. Birds chirped and fairy lights filled the sky.

Suddenly, I felt like I was being watched. Not the normal prickling sensation of the audience watching, but something else. In fact, I couldn't sense the audience at all.

Tarron.

It had to be. He made it so they couldn't see.

I stood and spun in a circle. "You're spying on me and it's creepy."

"Hardly spying." He stepped out from behind a tree about fifteen feet away. "Just enjoying the view."

"And I'm the view?"

He shrugged, an elegant gesture that somehow only made him look more deadly.

"You tried to keep me from reaching the Finfolk. Why?"

"I didn't try to stop you."

"You lied to me about their location, then you created the wind that made it nearly impossible to approach. If I hadn't been able to transport, I wouldn't have made it. Why are you trying to stop me?"

He prowled closer, moving swiftly and gracefully until he stood right in front of me. "Being the king is boring. This is entertaining."

There was *no* way he did things just for entertainment. This was a man with a mission. The way he held himself, the way he spoke, his constant alertness. "No, you're after something."

He was trying to figure out why he felt so strongly about me, but he also had ulterior motives. I could feel it.

He should be sitting in the stands, watching. But he wasn't. He was manipulating the competition. Trying to manipulate me.

I shifted back from him, wary as a cat and hating myself for the attraction that made my heart race and pulse pound. The tension that tightened the air made my head fog. It was an electric current that lit me up and was impossible to ignore. What was it between us that made it like this?

He might have felt the fated mate connection when we'd first met, but did that mean I should feel it as well?

"What is it about you?" he murmured.

My gaze moved to his lips.

No.

I took one more step back, bumping into the tree trunk and wincing again at the pain in my ribs.

"What's wrong?" he asked.

"Nothing."

"You're injured."

"Just a rib. That lion hit me pretty hard."

His green eyes glinted with concern. "I can heal it if you'll let me."

I frowned, debating. "Healing power?"

He nodded. "It's common among the Fae."

He would probably have to touch me to heal me. That's how it usually worked. I wanted him to touch me. For all the wrong reasons.

But it would be nice for my ribs not to hurt.

That was a good reason, right?

And I was protected by my spell. He hadn't realized I was his *Mograh* when he'd picked me up out of the lake.

I drew in a deep breath. "Okay."

He held out his hands, reaching slowly toward me. As if he knew I was the type to bite if someone touched me unexpectedly.

He was right about that.

"Which side?" he asked.

"The right."

When his hands landed on my ribs, I stifled a gasp. His touch was warm and sure, his hands strong. When he began to feed healing energy into me, my skin tingled all over.

The pain faded as he worked, replaced by intense awareness of his touch. The magic created a connection between us. I could almost feel his intention to make me better.

I shook my head.

Wishful thinking.

"Better?" he asked. His scent wrapped around me, and I breathed it in. Fresh water and the forest. And something masculine that was unidentifiable.

"Better." I almost vibrated from my desire to lean into

him and press my lips to his. What was it about this guy? I'd never felt like this with anyone. He must have had some kind of ability to enchant or hypnotize, because his words made my head go slightly fuzzy.

No. Dangerous.

But I wanted him so badly.

He'd saved my life.

All I could see were his lips and eyes. I swayed toward him, unable to resist.

His mouth pressed to mine, hard and fierce despite the softness of his lips. It was a magical combination that made my breath go short and my skin tingle.

His hands came up to wrap around my waist, strong and firm. He pressed me back against the tree, pinning me. I moaned, desire shooting through me. He was an expert at this, and I could feel every inch of his hard body against mine. He towered over me, and something purred to life inside me.

An awareness.

A connection.

As my head spun, his heat seeped into me, making my heart race. I shifted so I could run my hands over the broad planes of his back.

He growled low in his throat and pulled me closer, his lips dropping to my neck. He ran his tongue along my skin, making a shiver race through me. He bit down, and I cried out.

I wanted to tear off my clothes. From the way his hands were moving beneath the back of my shirt, trailing sparks across my flesh, I thought that he might want to do the same.

Abruptly, he pulled back.

I gasped, my gaze flashing up to his.

"You." His eyes flashed with shock. They were entirely black, as if he'd begun to shift as he had last time we'd kissed. "It's you."

Horror plunged me into cold water.

Shit.

I'd forgotten.

I'd *forgotten.* "I have no idea what you're talking about."

"You don't look the same, but I've kissed you before. Recently."

Oh fuck.

"You've taken off your makeup, and your hair is different." His gaze dropped to my chest. "Less of that as well."

"I have *no* idea what you're talking about."

"Don't play dumb." His gaze moved over my face. "You thought you were hidden from me. I can see it now. Your Mordaca disguise did an excellent job."

I scoffed.

"How did you hide the fact that you are my *Mograh*?" he asked. "I should have been able to sense you."

"So you'll admit it now?" He hadn't when I'd asked him about it in my workshop.

"It doesn't matter to me. I'm not looking for that."

"So you'll just ignore it."

"I'm sure as hell going to try."

Because I was a Dragon Blood. I deserved a medal for

being so stupid. I'd gotten so used to him here in the woods. He didn't seem quite like the suit-wearing king who'd come to me for the amplification charm two days ago.

My spell and disguise had worked so well that I'd just forgotten.

Moron.

What would it cost me?

I glanced at him, wondering if I could take him out.

"Thinking about trying to kill me, Dragon Blood?" he asked. "Make sure the information dies with me?"

I scowled at him, irritation rising within me. I lashed out, saying the worst thing I could think of about him. "You killed your brother."

Something flashed in his eyes. Pain?

I couldn't tell.

"I did," he said, making no excuse. But his face closed up and his eyes turned dark. "I'll be going now."

With that, he disappeared.

I sank back against the tree, gasping.

Idiot. He might have saved my life, but he'd killed his brother. And he'd done everything he could to get me out of this competition. He was dangerous, and I'd been a fool driven by attraction and my own cockiness that my disguise would hide me.

I'd been wrong. And I'd been wrong to trust him—even if it'd been just for a moment.

∽

After an uncomfortable night's sleep on a sleeping pad in the woods, I rose in the near-dark to the sound of morning birds.

Groggy, I sat up and rubbed a hand over my face.

Memories of Tarron haunted me, but there was nothing I could do about them now. Dawn was coming, and I needed to get a move on.

As soon as I had the Wish Stone, and a way to get rid of the crystal obelisk, I'd interrogate the hell out of Tarron. I wanted to know what he had to do with it and what he planned to do *about* it. Then I'd deal with the fact that he knew I was a Dragon Blood.

I turned to face the stone circle. The sky was turning from black to blue. The sun would come over the horizon soon. I dug into my pocket and pulled out the golden charm, then started toward the middle of the stone circle.

Magic sparked against my skin as I stepped inside. Quickly, I climbed to the top of the center stone and put the golden charm in place.

There were already two there, each with a little protective barrier of magic covering them.

I looked around, searching the forest nearby. The other two competitors were out there somewhere. They'd laid down their keys before me and hidden themselves away.

I hopped down and brushed off my hands. At least I knew what I was up against. Luna the Fae and Cardin the fire mage, whom I didn't know or care to know.

As the sun rose, I waited at the edge of the stone circle.

Every second that passed made tension tighten within me. This was it.

When the sun broke over the mountains at the horizon, one piercing beam of light struck the golden keys at the top of the center stone. Magic sparked on the air, and the bright glow nearly blinded me. It expanded outward, gleaming molten in the middle.

A portal.

I sprinted for it, spotting the other two competitors running from the other edges of the circle. I put on a burst of speed, grateful for my Dragon Blood. I plunged into the portal, and the ether sucked me in, spinning me through space toward places unknown.

12

THE ETHER SPAT ME OUT ON A HUGE BEACH MADE OF GRAY pebbles. The ocean sparkled blue and bright at the edge, and three boats sat on the shore. There was an island in the distance.

We needed to get there. It all but glowed with promise, and even my seeker sense tugged me toward it.

I sprinted for the closest boat, glancing behind me in time to see Luna pop out of the portal. The fire mage appeared next, then Tarron, appearing just as the portal snapped out of existence.

Tarron.

That stalker.

What was he doing?

I turned back and raced for the boat, then shoved it into the water and leapt on board. I grabbed the two oars and began to row. I had a head start of a few yards and was determined to keep it. Luna reached her boat and took off.

A half second later, Tarron leapt into the stern of her boat. She didn't complain, just kept rowing.

What the hell?

He was so not just here for the entertainment.

Could the audience see him?

Clearly things were getting weird, because Tarron was helping Luna. Or just hitching a ride in a contest he had no part in.

Cardin the fire mage leapt into his boat and took off with powerful strokes with the oars. The bastard looked strong. He was almost as big as Tarron, with fire red hair and black eyes that burned with the intense light of competition.

I pulled on the oars, using my increased strength to try to keep my lead. Tarron held out his hand, and a blast of wind hit my back. It pushed my boat in the water, killing any lead I'd gained.

Luna and the fire mage were pulling up alongside. I looked behind me to see if the island was close.

Shit.

Miles away yet, and I was losing ground.

And there was no way I could keep up this speed with Tarron blasting me with wind.

I scowled at him and shouted, "You're a bastard."

It was personal now. Normally I'd just kick ass, but if I was wasting time slinging insults, it meant I was *pissed*.

Should I hit him with a potion bomb?

But he was the king. Would he disqualify me? *Could* he?

He'd killed his own brother, so yeah, anything was possible.

No, there were other ways to do this. Surreptitiously, I sliced my thumb with my fingernail. Blood welled and pain smarted. He already knew what I was, but I still wanted to be subtle, just in case the audience was watching. I needed just a little bit of new magic, just a little bit of an advantage...

I called upon my Dragon Blood, envisioning the power of water. The ocean surged around us, and I focused on it. Soon, I could feel it beneath the boat. Feel the force and power of it. I commanded it to push my boat ahead.

The vessel jumped forward. It fought against Tarron's howling gale, and I poured more magic into it. The boat won out, pushing through the water. I pulled into the lead again, gaining by several yards. Then a dozen.

The fire mage shouted, irritation in his cry. He raised a hand and shot a fireball right at me.

"Shit!" I hurled the oars into the boat and called upon a shield from the ether, lunging it in front of the fireball before it smashed into the bow. The force of the blow shook my arms, and I shuddered.

I couldn't row and defend at the same time, so I used my magic to propel the boat forward. It took so much power that my strength began to flag, but I pushed on.

The fire mage continued to throw his blasts in between strokes of his oars. He nearly hit me a half dozen times, but I was quick with my shield. Every time the fire slammed into it, my arms shook. I gritted my teeth.

At one point, Tarron blasted him with wind as well, trying to force him back.

Because the mage had to contend with the Tarron's howling wind, Luna pulled into the lead ahead of him.

I was barely able to keep my lead, and by the time I neared the shore, my magic was nearly tapped out. When my little boat finally surged up onto the beach, I jumped out without a backward glance. Luna and Tarron were only seconds behind, with the fire mage close after.

I sprinted up the beach and past the dunes, reaching a massive field. There was only one thing on the island—a grove of trees, right in the middle. My seeker sense dragged me toward it. I tried to transport, but a spell blocked me. So I ran for it, pushing myself as hard as I could.

Tarron reached my side and kept up easily. I pushed myself hard, sprinting as fast as I could. I looked back and spotted Luna. The Fae was fast, and she *did* have wings. Beautiful blue ones that carried her swiftly through the sky.

Shit.

She was catching up too. I sucked a breath into my burning lungs and ran faster, headed for the grove of trees. Rowan trees, just like the seer had said.

I reached the tree line just as Tarron and Luna did. She landed and ran in alongside us. I dodged trunks and leapt over fallen limbs, heading for the powerful magic that I could feel within the glen. It pulled at me, beckoning me nearer.

On foot, I was faster than Luna, taking the lead. Tarron kept up without trouble, which irritated the hell out of me. He tried to trip me twice, but I was too quick, leaping over the roots that he forced out of the ground. Finally, we spilled out into a huge clearing bordered on all sides by more rowan trees.

In the middle of the clearing stood the biggest tree I'd ever seen. The ones in the Fae realm were huge, of course, but they were taller than they were wide. This was a rowan tree that had to be hundreds of feet tall *and* wide.

The magic was coming from it, though I had no idea what to do.

Then the earth beneath my feet began to shake. I stumbled, grabbing onto a tree limb for support. The earth around the huge rowan broke apart, and it began to rise up, revealing the roots. They twisted and turned through the ground, and as the tree rose, they formed holes and divots big enough that a person could climb in. One even looked like a tunnel. Magic billowed out from the earth.

We were supposed to go in there. There was no question.

As the tree rose up, so, too, did new creatures. Monsters formed of tree roots and dirt climbed out of the ground. Some had three legs, some had four. All were totally unrecognizable. Each had two eyes made of dark black gems, and they turned them toward us.

Shit.

I called upon my bow and arrow, though I had my doubts about their effectiveness.

The creatures roared and charged, at least a dozen of them. I fired three arrows in quick succession, aiming for the first dirt monster. The arrows slammed into the beast, but it kept running.

As I'd thought.

I stashed the weapon away and called upon a baseball bat. I rarely used it, but for close-range attacks against magical creatures that needed to be smashed into oblivion, it usually worked like a charm.

I charged the nearest one, raising the bat high. The monster ran on three legs made of twigs and dirt, its black gemstone eyes riveted to me. A mouth full of thorns gaped wide, and each brown point dripped with yellow liquid.

Some kind of toxin, probably.

I reached the monster and slammed my baseball bat against its head. The dirt and twigs blasted apart, flying everywhere. Toxin-tipped thorns flew through the air, crashing into the dirt. For good measure, I smacked my bat down onto the beast's back, sending it into the ground.

As soon as it was down, I spun, looking for another. An even bigger one was nearly to me, its front claws made of thorns as long as my hand. I raised my bat and smashed it into the creature's head, but it was going too fast.

As the head exploded, the rest of the body slammed into me, plowing me to the ground. Claws somehow managed to rake across me, and I screamed. The creature had buried me under a huge pile of dirt and twigs. Panic flared as I dropped the bat and scrambled up through the dirt and rocks that the monster had broken apart. I reached the surface and gasped for air, then climbed out.

To my left, Luna was battling her own monster, while the fire mage was unsuccessfully trying to fend off another. Tarron had taken out two. He was closer to the tree, both stronger and faster than the rest of us. He was definitely in the competition now, fighting for the prize just like we were.

But why?

There was no time to think about it. I needed my weapon if I was going to get to the tree.

The edge of my bat stuck out from the pile of wood and dirt that had once been the monster, and I grabbed it, then sprinted for the huge tree. Another beast came for me, but I was quicker this time, taking it out with two strikes.

I was nearly to the underground entrance when a shriek sounded from behind me.

I turned back to see the fire mage get his head bitten off by a huge dirt monster. The mage's body dipped limply to the ground.

Yuck.

Near the tree, Tarron fought four beasts that had leapt up. He moved so fast and so powerfully that it was hard to keep track of him as he tore them apart.

I looked away, catching sight of two more monsters headed toward me. Shit. They were fast, and two was a problem. I readied my bat, heart thundering and muscles aching. The beasts hurtled closer, their enormous mouths gaping open to display mouths full of fangs. They were so close together that I wouldn't be able to hit both at the same time.

At least one would reach me.

From out of nowhere, the thorn wolf appeared. He plowed into the closest beast, taking him down in a pile of woody limbs.

The other monster kept coming for me, and I raised my bat, slamming it into its face. I leapt out of the way as the body tumbled forward, then jumped over the carcass and sprinted for the entrance into the tree's root system.

The thorn wolf took out any beast that approached me, and he was the only reason I managed to gain a lead against Tarron, who was fighting more monsters that had appeared.

Magic flowed out of the tunnel, beckoning me forward. My lungs heaved as I ran for it, leaping over raised roots that had broken through the surface of the ground.

Cool air enveloped me as I sprinted into the darkness. A few feet later, fairy lights flared to life, illuminating the interior. Huge roots shot through the dirt around me, and the tunnel widened as I went deeper.

Footsteps sounded from behind me, and I turned back to see Tarron. He sprinted after me, green eyes intense.

I ran forward, putting on as much speed as I could. I didn't know exactly what I was running toward, but I knew I was close to the end. I could feel it in the air. A tension. An expectancy. The prize was within this tree, and damned if I wasn't going to get it.

I'd have to beat Tarron, though, because clearly, he was

after it too.

I know it.

A few seconds later, I entered an enormous cavern beneath the earth. It sparkled blue and bright, and I realized that it was gemstones stuck within the ground that gave it the sparkling color. Emeralds and sapphires, just blanketing the earth.

Wow.

I skidded to halt, taking in my surroundings. Right in the middle of the space was a pedestal made of beautiful white stone. A simple carved stone ball sat on top of it, sparking with magic.

The prize.

No question.

Tarron's footsteps thundered behind me. He was almost to me.

I raced forward, careful to try to sense the type of magic that I was approaching. It filled the air, thick and intense. It felt almost like breathing in hot lavender tea, and I slowed my steps. I needed to beat Tarron to the prize, but I didn't need to end up dead because I'd missed something important.

I breathed shallowly, carefully avoiding the gemstones studded in the ground as I approached the pedestal. As I neared it, the air thickened even more.

Spirits drifted up from the gems, ghostlike figures that crowded around me. They glowed green and blue, their features indistinct. In a way, they reminded me of Agatha.

They reached toward me with spectral hands, and I

stopped.

The energy drifting from them wasn't dark. It pricked fiercely against my skin, but not in a bad way. In a protective way.

This was a protection charm, not unlike the ones I'd installed underneath my house to protect the Well of Power.

I stilled, letting them get a feel for me. I imagined my intentions, trying to send the message that I meant no ill will. *I will do no harm with the prize. I will use it for good.*

A faint tinge of grief hit me that I might not be able to use it to figure out what my true second species was. Apparently, that was more important to me than I'd let myself believe. All these years I'd repressed the desire, and something about visiting the Fae realm made it rise up in me.

But there were bigger things at risk here. Like the fate of the Fae realm. I needed this prize to help them.

The ghosts around me seemed to vibrate as they absorbed the information and processed it. I tried to get a feel for where Tarron and Luna were, but I couldn't. The ghosts surrounded me too closely.

Finally, they withdrew their hands. I gasped, sagging in relief, then hurried forward. Tension tightened my muscles as I caught sight of the prize, still sitting on the pedestal. It glowed bright and promising, a perfect sphere imbued with incredible magic.

I stopped in front of it, then hovered my hand over the top.

No protective magic prickled. I got no sense of any danger at all, in fact.

I picked it up, grinning at the weight of it in my palm, then turned.

Tarron grabbed me, his arms going around my waist. For the briefest second, a connection flared between us.

I liked his arms around me. I couldn't help it.

Fated mates.

It didn't matter. We were enemies.

"No!" I thrashed and struggled, trying to break free. I managed to twist around until my back was to his chest, but he yanked me tighter to him.

Shit.

I kicked back, trying to hit his knee, but I missed. Panicked, I sliced my finger with my thumbnail, letting the blood well. I imagined new magic, and power that would allow me to—

Luna appeared as if out of nowhere, her blue hair shining. She grabbed the prize and yanked it away from me.

I expected Tarron to release me and go for her, but he didn't. I lunged toward the prize, but he held me tight.

"What the hell is going on?" I demanded, calling upon a magic that would freeze the blood in their veins. I'd never created that kind of magic before—wasn't even sure if it was possible—but damned if I didn't want to try.

"Sorry, can't tell you." Luna crossed her arms over her chest.

Tarron kept his grip on me, making no move to take the prize from Luna.

Understanding dawned. "You two have been in on it together all along." Luna must have lied about her origin to throw me off the scent. "But why? What's going on?"

There was silence. I could feel Tarron debating what to do with me. It could go either direction.

Right now, he was clearly deciding if he was going to take me out of the picture.

There was no one watching down here, just his minion. Luna had seemed like a bubble-headed Fae with some reasonable magic. She was far more, apparently.

But he was hesitating. He didn't want to.

And there was no reason to hide my cards anymore. He knew who I was, what I was. That I had ulterior motives, though he didn't quite understand them yet. I had nothing left to lose, so I might as well ask. I'd wanted to play it sneaky and win and figure out what was going on that way, but the shit had hit the fan on that plan.

"What's going on in the King's Grove?" I demanded. "This has to do with the demonic energy there, doesn't it?" There was no way two such huge events weren't connected.

Tarron stiffened. Luna frowned.

"You can tell me." I struggled harder in Tarron's grip. "I've been there. I've seen it."

"Not demonic energy," Tarron said.

I stopped struggling. "What?"

"Unseelie Fae."

Oh, shit. I hadn't seen that coming. Though they were the dark version of the Seelie Fae—perhaps their energy could read as demonic.

"You've gotten in the middle of something you don't understand," Luna said.

"I understand enough." I finally landed a blow on Tarron's foot, and he let me go, though I had a feeling he was actually kind of ready to.

He stepped around to join Luna, both of them squaring off against me. My gaze went to the stone ball in Luna's hands, but this had become way more complicated than me just grabbing the thing and wishing for the demonic energy to go away.

"What do you think you understand?" Tarron's voice was cold, but intrigued.

"There's dark energy coming from that crystal obelisk in the King's Grove. I thought it was demonic, but apparently it's Unseelie Fae."

Luna spit when I said their name. She must really hate them.

And my mother might be one of them. Was she really connected to this, or was it just coincidence? Though my mind went immediately there, I didn't have time to focus on that now. "I think it has something to do with all of the deaths that happened a couple months ago. I was sent here to stop it before it causes any more."

Tarron nodded, understanding dawning. "You're from the Council of Demon Slayers."

"Yes. You denied to their faces that there was a problem. Are you in league with them?"

"No. I denied that there was demon energy infiltrating my realm."

"You denied our help. So are you in league with them?" I repeated.

"*No.* I am not. And what good are demon hunters against an invasion of the Unseelie Fae? You know nothing about them. Nothing about the problem. We didn't want your help or need it."

"That doesn't mean I can't help."

"And that's why you entered the competition?" Luna asked. "To help?"

"To spy on him." I pointed to Tarron. "And figure out what he's doing with the magic in the King's Grove. And how to stop it."

"He *is* trying to stop it," Luna said.

"Then why don't more Fae know it's a problem? You're keeping it a secret."

"It's complicated." Tarron gritted out the words.

"We don't need people to panic," Luna said. "If people panic, our realm is weakened."

"They really just don't notice it?" I asked. "It makes your realm reek of dark magic. I can even see it."

"They've been enchanted not to notice it," Tarron said. "Most of them. There is a team of Fae who know what's going on, and we're fixing it."

"We have a plan, and so far, it's going perfectly," Luna said.

"What kind of plan?"

"We can't just wish the energy away, if that's what you're suggesting," Tarron said.

"But you'll use that orb to fix things?"

"You're asking too many questions," Tarron said, irritation in his voice.

Suddenly, my predicament became clear.

Here I was, deep beneath a tree at the heart of the Fae realm, my cover blown. I was entirely at his mercy.

As if sensing the change in the atmosphere, the earth rumbled.

I jumped, looking around. "What was that?"

"The tree is sinking," Tarron said. "Come on."

My heart jumped. Sinking?

Shit. We'd be buried alive.

I tried my transport magic, but it didn't work. Blocked like before.

Tarron grabbed my hand and pulled me forward.

Together, the three of us raced from the cavern. The tunnels shook as we sprinted through, and my heart thundered in my ears. Dirt rained down on my head, and my lungs burned as I ran, panic driving me. Being buried alive seemed like the worst way to go.

Luna and Tarron were as fast as I was, thankfully, and we made it out of the underground lair just as the tree roots sank back into the earth.

I stood at the base of the tree, panting. The sun shined brightly, and I shielded my face to inspect the area around us. The root monsters were gone, thank fates. Fae officials had arrived, a half dozen of them dressed in crimson and gold outfits. Two were dealing with the body of the mage, and the other four started toward us.

Tarron looked at Luna. "Go hold them off, would you?"

She nodded and handed him the orb, which he took.

"Who are they?" I asked.

"Part of my Royal Guard. They've been manipulating the way that the audience sees the competition."

"So they don't know that you're involved. What you're really up to."

"They can't."

"I think they could handle it, you know. You don't have to treat them like glass."

"I'm going to fix it, and it won't be an issue."

Somehow, I thought there was more to it than he was letting on. In fact, I was sure of it. "What are you hiding?"

"Nothing."

I stared hard at him. In the distance, the officials were arguing with Luna. Clearly, they wanted to approach the king. We only had seconds.

I had to decide.

Was he really working in the best interest of his kingdom, and therefore the world? Because if the dark energy enveloped the Fae realm, Agatha had said that it would move to earth next.

There was so much at stake. Could I trust him?

"Why are you hosting a magical competition in the middle of a crisis? What do you want the prize for?"

"The sacred Rowan Grove only opens during this competition. It is where the Wish Stone is kept, and we'll use it to help us destroy the obelisk."

"Well, go ahead, then. Wish it away. Make it all better."

He gave me a look that suggested I was a moron. "It's not that simple."

"It never is. How can I trust you?"

"You don't have a choice," he said. "I could kill you here —and I would, if I thought you were here to harm my people—and none of my guard would say a thing. You signed your life away when you entered this competition."

"You can't kill me. You saved me from the Finfolk."

His mouth hardened. "I did. I had to. I didn't understand why then, but I do now." His fists clenched. "But hear me clearly—I *could* kill you, even if you are my *Mograh*. It might tear my soul apart, but to protect my people, I would."

Tear his soul apart?

Was that what happened when you lost your *Mograh*?

Not that he even wanted one. He'd made that clear. He planned to ignore it.

But as for the threats, I believed him. He was killer. He'd killed his brother, after all. The people in the village whispered that he was cruel. A murderous usurper.

But I trusted him—at least in this. Like he said, I had to. He was trying to save his people, even though they didn't know it.

The Royal Guard was coming, and it was just me against them. Me against the king.

"Fine," I said. "I trust that you mean well. But I want to help."

13

THE REST OF THE DAY HAPPENED IN A BLUR. TARRON HAD kept me close to his side as we headed back to the Seelie realm. During the closing ceremonies, Luna appeared on stage as the winner, and I'd stood by in the shadows.

It'd worked perfectly, since I'd wanted to stay out of the limelight and she was a fantastic actress. Being a skilled liar helped, definitely.

I couldn't help but smile slightly at the glowing grin on her face as she waved at the crowd, clutching the carved Wish Stone to her chest. I'd seen her in action. The blue-haired, pink-eyed Fae could turn serious in an instant, and this was all an act. She did a better job than I ever would have.

After the ceremonies, I'd been led to my room, always under guard. I still hadn't had a chance to speak to Tarron privately, but he'd agreed to let me attend the meeting tonight in the war room where they would plan their attack on the crystal obelisk. I wanted to be in on the action and he knew it, but he didn't quite trust me yet.

Fair enough, since I didn't trust him either.

After a quick meal that had been delivered by a slender Fae man, I'd reapplied my usual makeup and hair. The bouffant wasn't quite as high as normal—just slightly higher in the front—but I liked it because it made me look badass. What had started as a disguise had become part of me.

For good measure, I pulled my zipper down to reveal a bit of cleavage, then nodded.

There. I looked like myself again. There was no point in hiding what I was, now that the king knew. If he wanted to tell the world what I was, I couldn't use this disguise anymore anyway.

With the silence of the room pressing in on me, I couldn't help but think about Tarron. About what he knew of me. About the secrets he still held. About the fact that I was his *Mograh* and we were both going to ignore it. He was struggling to, though. I could sense it.

I popped a butterscotch hard candy in my mouth and tried to resist chewing it.

A knock sounded at the door, and I went to open it. Luna stood on the other side. She was dressed in the red and gold uniform of the Royal Guard, her blue hair pulled up in a series of complicated braids.

"Don't you clean up well?" I said.

She did a mocking curtsy, then said, "It's time."

She led me up through the castle, which was as light

and airy as ever. There was a cool night breeze drifting through the open windows, carrying with it the sound of revelry from outside. Diaphanous window coverings fluttered in the breeze, giving the place an enchanted fairytale vibe.

A group of Fae women hurried by, their colorful gowns trailing behind them. They were the same group I'd seen before.

We passed a wall made entirely of sparkling water, and another constructed of intricately braided tree limbs. Birds nested among the branches, snoozing quietly.

Luna led me into the war room. It was long and rectangular, with a massive table in the middle. The towering ceiling was painted with scenes of battle, and the table itself was covered with a huge three-dimensional plan of the King's Grove.

Tarron stood at the head of the table, leaning over the plan. He still wore the dirty clothes from earlier, and his eyes looked tired.

Ten Fae stood around him, all dressed in the red and gold that Luna wore. An older woman sat in one of the chairs, her pale white hair a perfect halo around her head. The silver dress she wore sparkled with light, and her hands rested precisely on the arms of her chair.

I leaned toward Luna and murmured, "This is it? There aren't more of you?"

Luna shifted toward me to answer, but Tarron spoke in her place. Damn, I'd forgotten about his hearing.

"Twelve is the maximum number that we can protect

against the crystal obelisk's dark enchantment." He looked at the older woman. "Arrowen is a seer. She's able to help us plan our attack."

I met his gaze, which traveled from my hair to my chest. Something flickered in his eyes. Interest?

Did he prefer my Elvira look?

There was no time to think of that now. I inspected everyone in the room, trying to get a feel for them. They clearly weren't here to ambush me, so Tarron must have been telling the truth.

We were going to try to take out the obelisk. I didn't dare mention the fact that my mother's signature was similar to the one that the obelisk emitted. If I found something, I found something. But no way in hell I'd admit to that.

"What have I missed?" I asked.

"Not much." He pointed to the map. "We were discussing how the troops would provide backup as I go to deploy the bomb beneath the crystal obelisk. I need to get to the base of the Unseelie obelisk, or it won't work."

"The Unseelie Fae will defend their incursion," Arrowen said. "You can expect them to appear in great numbers if you get too close. It will be a true fight."

"How did the incursion start?" I asked. "Did the obelisk just appear one day?"

"Yes. Several months ago, the stone appeared in the King's Grove," Tarron said. "It plunged up through the earth. At the time, the dark magic wasn't as strong. It takes time to grow. For a while, we didn't know where it came from. It was Arrowen who was able to see what the Unseelie Fae were attempting."

"They are attempting to destroy our kingdom and all of the Seelie Fae," Arrowen said. "The obelisk compels any who approach it to kill their brethren."

"And it worked," I said. "Considering that ten percent of your population disappeared. But why would they want to kill you?"

"We don't know," Tarron said. "For a long time, we existed in harmony. We never liked each other, but we're two sides of the Fae coin. Light and dark, good and evil."

"But it's never as cut and dry as that," I said.

"True. They have some good qualities, and we have some bad," Luna said. "Recently, one of their bad qualities is that they are launching a quiet attack on our realm."

Tarron nodded. "But we now have a way to stop it. We've been working on it for the last month, and we've gotten the final piece of the puzzle."

He had to mean the Wish Stone. But no one mentioned his brother, I realized. He would have been king when the stone first appeared. Had Tarron used his brother's distraction over that as an opportunity to kill him and take his throne?

I studied the Fae.

He was ruthless. He could be cold.

But somehow, I doubted it.

Tarron walked to a small table against the wall and retrieved three objects. He returned to Arrowen and set them on the table—the carved rock that was the Wish

Stone, the amplification charm that I'd made in my shop not so long ago, and a brilliant red orb about the size of a baseball. Crimson light flashed within, looking like lightning. "These are the tools that you commanded we find." He looked up at me. "They are the key to destroying the stone and cutting off the Unseelie Fae from this realm."

Arrowen leaned closer, an intent look on her face. She raised a delicate hand and hovered it over the Wish Stone first. A satisfied expression crossed her features. "Yes. This will allow you to make a dozen people immune to the Unseelie obelisk's dark power."

"It's too weak to wish the power away?" I asked.

"Not too weak, exactly." Her pale blue eyes met mine. "The obelisk is created from dark Unseelie magic. The Wish Stone is made of light Seelie magic. They counteract each other."

"Ah, too bad."

She moved her hand to the glowing red ball and hovered it over the top. She raised her other hand and let it rest on the amplifying charm I'd created.

She frowned, her gaze flicking up to Tarron. "Not strong enough."

"What?" His eyes flashed. "It's the most powerful magical bomb in the world. With the most powerful amplifying charm."

Ah, so that's what he'd wanted my amplifying charm for.

"Still, we knew it was a risk," Arrowen said.

"What's the problem?" I asked. "My charm isn't strong enough?"

"The bomb isn't either," Tarron said. "We knew it wouldn't be, so we hoped to amplify its destructive magic."

"It will do great damage," Arrowen said. "But I'm afraid that unless you can destroy the entire obelisk, some of the dark magic will remain."

I remembered how powerful that magic was. The compulsion to kill had nearly eaten me alive. If it hadn't been for the thorn wolf dragging me out of there, I might have succumbed.

"Two bombs?" Luna asked.

"There's only one like that in the world," Tarron said. "I had to steal it from the Underworld."

Ah. A memory pinged. Aeri's boyfriend, Declan, had been sent by the High Court of the Angels to find the stolen bomb. Apparently he hadn't found it, probably because it was protected in this realm.

"We could get more bombs," Luna said. "Smaller ones, but lots of them."

"That wouldn't do it." Tarron frowned, studying the collection of objects in front of Arrowen. "The big bomb would absorb the power of the smaller ones. We need one enormous explosion from one source."

"And amplification is the only way to do it." I held my hand out to Arrowen. "Am I strong enough?"

She flicked her gaze up to me, then gripped my hand. Her magic flowed through me, feathery and soft. I could feel her testing my powers.

Her brow wrinkled. "Yes, if you add it to the amplification charm that you made."

"You can tell I made it?" I asked.

"The magic feels the same."

I nodded, then looked at Tarron. "Among other things, I'm an amplifier. I can make your bomb stronger if I go with you when you deploy it."

He frowned at me. "I may not make it out alive."

I looked around the group of crimson-robed guards, then out the window. The sound of revelry still drifted from outside. These people deserved to live. Not only that, if the dark magic devoured this realm, it would move to earth next.

There was really no choice.

Decided, I met Tarron's gaze. "On three conditions."

"Two?" He raised a brow.

"I'd literally be saving your kingdom. I don't think three is too much to ask."

"You will have your three conditions."

"You don't need to know what they are first?"

"As you said, without you, I will have no kingdom. And we will all be dead. Or refugees to earth. So no, I do not need to know what they are."

"You will begin your attack tomorrow morning," Arrowen said. "The Unseelie Fae are weakest then."

There was a bit more planning for logistics, then everyone departed. I turned to face Tarron.

He waited for me by the window.

Memories of our kisses flashed in my mind's eye. There

was so much attraction and mistrust here that it tangled up my feelings. The fact that I was his *Mograh* didn't help matters. But until we fixed what was wrong here, none of that mattered.

His gaze met mine. "I suppose you'll tell me your conditions now?"

"I bet you can guess at least one of them."

"You don't want me to reveal your true nature to anyone."

"A blood oath on it, yes." I approached him and stopped a few feet away. Moonlight gleamed on his face, setting it in shadows that made him look even more mysterious. "How did you figure out what I was, anyway? Is that a Fae talent?"

"Not all Fae. And I wasn't prying. Not intentionally. Dragon Blood is very easy to detect."

The memory of him licking the blood from his fang flared in my mind, and my heart beat a little faster.

No. Stupid. I couldn't become infatuated again. Two kisses was two too many, especially with ruthless Fae royalty that I didn't trust. "Have you ever met another of my kind?"

"Once. They're dead now."

"Because you told the world what they were?"

His expression turned dark. "No. I wouldn't."

"Then swear on it." I called a silver blade from the ether and handed it to him.

He took the blade without hesitation. "What must I do?"

"Slice your finger. Then I will slice mine. We will grip arms, and when our forearms touch, our blood will mingle. I will create a spell that will rot your tongue if you ever speak of what I am or say anything that would harm me. Or my sister."

His brows rose. "Effective."

"Very. But it requires consent."

"You only practice blood magic with consent."

"I may live in Darklane, but I'm not a dark magic practitioner. Not in that way, at least."

He nodded and sliced his finger. Red blood welled. I pulled up my sleeve, then I sliced by own finger with my thumbnail. We reached out and gripped forearms, and I tried to ignore the strength of his muscles beneath my grip. The heat of his touch.

His warm blood smeared my skin, and mine slicked his. I met his gaze and began the chant, feeding my magic into his body through the touch of my blood. Tension sparked between us, heat and fire. It had nothing to do with the spell, and I had to force my mind away from it.

I drew in a breath, and began the spell. "Speak of me, regret will be. Upon your life with blood intact, you will never speak of me nor break this pact."

Magic sparked on the air, flowing through the two of us, then faded. I let go of his arm, my own skin chilling. "And that's that."

He nodded. "Your secret is safe." He met my gaze. "Though it was safe before."

"Good." It would be a nice world if I could have trusted

him. But I didn't live in that world. I never had. "The next one is simple. I want my sister at the battle tomorrow. Someone to have my back. And frankly, you could use her. She's immensely powerful."

He nodded. "Fine."

"That was easy."

"What was your other condition?"

"Tell me about your brother."

Dark shadows crossed his face, and he stepped back.

"Well?" I prodded.

"I killed him for his throne."

"And?"

"And, that's what I did. I am king now." He crossed his arms, his expression and energy suddenly icy.

"That's what you tell your entire Court. All your subjects," I said. "That's not what I'm interested in. I want the truth."

"The truth is that I killed him. He was a good ruler, but I knew that I would be a better one." There was almost a hint of a lie to his voice. A discomfort that I could sense when he hesitated just slightly before the word *better*.

"This is part of my condition for helping you. I want the whole truth, because I don't think it's as simple as you say. He was alive when this stone appeared. When the murders happened. I want the truth that you're hiding from everyone."

His magic seemed to vibrate around him, tension and anger and pain. He stepped forward, gripping my arms and pulling me toward him. I gasped, my heart jumping.

"How do you read me so well?" he demanded, brow furrowed.

There was so much feeling inside him—somehow I could sense it, rioting inside me. Anguish. Rage.

It twisted something inside me, breaking open a part of my heart that had been hardened years ago. I shifted in his grasp, managing to get my arms around him to hug him.

I wasn't a hugger.

I was the exact opposite of a hugger.

Except something compelled me to this, and I couldn't stop. I wrapped my arms around him and tried to push as much good energy into him as I could. It was all nonsense. I didn't have that type of power. But I tried anyway.

Frankly, it felt weird as hell, but I didn't stop.

He stiffened even more in my arms, clearly confused.

Then he relaxed just slightly, dropping his head.

I glanced up, almost expecting to see tears on his cheek.

Of course there were none. This was not a man who cried. It'd probably do him some good, but it would never happen.

All the same, his expression looked shattered. It lasted only a fraction of a second, then it was gone. He closed himself right back up and stepped away. I could see nothing on his face but impassive self-control.

"Holding it all in—whatever it is—doesn't make you stronger," I said.

"Holding it all in is the only way I can function."

I stayed silent, waiting.

"My brother was a good man. A good king. Until he entered the King's Grove and found the Unseelie obelisk. We didn't realize what had happened at first, but it polluted his mind. He spent too long in its thrall, unable to escape."

Horror dawned, but not surprise. I'd almost guessed. "He killed the missing Fae. The ones who are mourned."

Tarron nodded his head sharply. "At first, when they disappeared, we thought it was voluntary. They had decided to leave. Then, too many went missing. And their remains began to turn up."

"You had no idea it was him?"

"At first, no. I never would have suspected it. I'm the one who discovered him sacrificing them in the Dark Grove. Their deaths made the obelisk stronger. It made the magic spread more quickly, and in turn, made my brother more insane."

Oh fates, this was terrible. "What did you do?"

"I tried to stop him. To reason with him." He shook his head, and it was clear it hadn't worked. "Finally, I captured him. By then, he'd killed over two hundred Fae. Arrowen helped me try to drive the dark magic from him. But the Unseelie curse was too strong." He said the word Unseelie as if it were the most disgusting thing in the world. "It was twisted throughout his body, too deeply embedded in his soul."

"You couldn't save him."

"We killed him. The process of trying to save him killed him."

His eyes darkened, their depths tortured. "And in a way, it was a blessing. Because I would have had to kill him if our attempted cure hadn't. He was too powerful. Too dangerous."

"And you told no one what he did."

"No one. Only Arrowen knows, though a couple of the King's Guard might suspect. I couldn't ruin his legacy. He was a good king. A good brother."

Shit. Just...shit.

That was awful. "And it's why you've told no one about the obelisk. You don't want them thinking any more about your brother, so that his legacy stays intact."

He nodded sharply.

"They all think you're an asshole."

He shrugged. "I am an asshole. The younger brother of the king who did all the work. I enjoyed my station. My power. My freedom. Everyone already thought I was an asshole—which I was—so it was easy to keep that going. Only natural."

Though I hated the idea that everyone thought he was an asshole, it wasn't my place to change things. Some people didn't need acknowledgment for their good deeds, and he was one of them. I wasn't the same—I wanted credit for the things I did—but I'd never been in his situation before. I'd probably do the same for Aeri.

"And your parents?" I asked.

"Dead, thankfully." He dragged a hand over his face. "I'd have hated for our mother to see what had become of us."

His brother had probably been the only person he'd ever cared for, then. And he'd killed him. Inadvertently, but he'd done it.

"The Fae still have to be wondering about the murders," I said. "It's only been a couple of months, but eventually, they'll want an answer."

"And we'll give them one. After we've destroyed the obelisk and we're safe, I'll explain it to them. Without mentioning my brother. I've already given the story to the Royal Guard. They seemed to believe it."

It wasn't the worst plan. They'd be able to blame the deaths on the dark magic without explicitly mentioning his brother. Tarron would still be the asshole usurper king, but he seemed to want it that way.

"This is for the best." His voice was suddenly brisk. "We will be protected tomorrow, but if the obelisk's curse takes me, you know what to do."

"Kill you." It was the only obvious thing. And suddenly, I wished I didn't know the truth. Because with everything that he'd told me, I realized that I was beginning to care for him.

14

I LEFT TARRON'S QUARTERS IMMEDIATELY AFTER OUR conversation. We didn't speak of the fact that I was his *Mograh,* though it had hung heavily on the air.

An hour later, a knock sounded on the door to my room, and I turned to open it.

Aeri stood on the other side, her pale waterfall of hair flowing over the shoulder of her white ghost suit. She'd come as soon as I'd called.

I hugged her. "I see you came prepared."

"You mentioned there might be a fight."

"Isn't there always?"

"Usually." She pulled back and studied me, her blue eyes intense. "Are you sure you're all right?"

I nodded.

"How did you keep your identity a secret from him?" She gestured to me. "Because right now, you're pretty obvious."

"He just figured me out, so there's no point in hiding anymore. But I had him fooled for a while."

"But he knows now."

"He does."

"Which means we'll have to kill him." There wasn't a hint of a joke in her voice. Aeri would commit regicide for me in a heartbeat. I'd do the same for her. In fact, I didn't want to think of what I'd do for her.

The little bit of darkness that had always existed in me roared to life at the thought. That darkness would take out legions of people to protect Aeri.

Somehow, I had a feeling she wouldn't approve of that.

"We don't. I got him to make a blood oath that he wouldn't reveal my secret or do anything to harm either of us."

"Do you trust him beyond that?"

"It doesn't matter if I do. I won't see him again."

"Despite the fact that he thinks you're his fated mate?"

"He's determined to ignore it."

"How do you feel about that?"

"Fine." *Lie.*

I didn't want to have my destiny determined by Fae magic and fate, but I felt something for him. It would be smart to ignore it, but I didn't want to.

I shoved the thoughts away and changed the subject. We sat on the bed, and I brought her up to speed with what she'd missed, including the missing bomb that Declan was hunting. I didn't know much about what we were up against—all I knew was that the Unseelie Fae were the evil ones and that the Seelie hated them—but then again, we often went into fights only partially prepared. We had the Fae at our side, at least.

I debated telling her about my mother, but it was late. We had only hours left, and I wasn't ready to face that yet.

That night, it was hard to sleep. Stress made me eat so many hard candies that I became ill, and the dreams were worse.

Dreams of Tarron killing his brother. Of me killing Tarron.

When I woke, I was desperate to get this over with. The battle would be dangerous—possibly deadly—but at least it would get my mind off things.

Aeri had spent the night with me in my giant lake of a bed, and we dressed in silence.

Aeri tugged on her boots and put her pale hair in a ponytail. She met my gaze. "Ready for this?"

I gave the mirror one last look. Hair, done. Eyes, done. Zipper, done. "War paint's ready. Let's go."

We left my quarters and headed to the war room. Everyone was there already, studying the three-dimensional plan of the King's Grove. I introduced Aeri, and we ran over the plan again.

Most of the team would attack from strategic points, holding off the Unseelie Fae that we expected to appear, while Tarron and I made our way beneath the obelisk. There was supposed to be a portal there, since the Unseelie Fae didn't technically live underground. They'd used some pretty serious magic to connect their two realms and send their destructive obelisk through.

I met Tarron's gaze just briefly, but we didn't speak. Now we each possessed the other's greatest secret. He was magically forbidden from speaking mine, but I wouldn't tell his either.

The twelve of us departed the war room fifteen minutes before sunrise. It didn't take long to make our way through the silent castle and toward the King's Grove. The dark magic that had rolled out from the place earlier had grown thicker in the time that I'd been away. It still reeked of brimstone and putrid night lilies, and my heartbeat thundered.

Aeri covered her mouth and grimaced. "That's awful."

"It is." And it might be the scent of my mother.

Fates, that was terrible.

I shoved the thought aside.

With the way that the magic was expanding, we were handling this just in time. Tarron wouldn't have been able to hide this from the citizens much longer.

Tarron held up his hand, and we stopped on command, then circled up. He held the Wish Stone in the center of the circle of people.

"Protect our minds from the dark power of the Unseelie obelisk." His voice rang with authority, and the carved rock glowed bright as it absorbed his commands. His gaze flicked around the circle. "Lay your hand upon the orb."

One by one, we reached out to touch the glowing

surface. When my fingertips pressed to it, magic sizzled up my arms and wrapped around my chest, shining bright. All around me, the Fae glowed as well. Warmth flowed through me.

Protection.

Suddenly, the stink of the dark magic didn't smell so bad.

Thank fates. If this hadn't worked, we'd have been screwed.

Once we were all protected, Tarron gave the orb to Luna, who tucked it into a pack on her back. He then strode ahead, approaching the gate with determined steps. He wore navy tactical wear—boots and sturdy pants with a dark chain-mail vest that was imbued with some kind of repelling magic. A small pack was strapped to his back. Within, he carried the bomb and the amplifier.

He touched the gate, then frowned, shooting me a look.

Whoops. When I'd broken in earlier, I hadn't been able to replace the spell that had protected it. "Sorry."

He turned back to the gate and unlocked it, then pushed it open. Dark magic billowed out, and I held my breath, muscles tense. It floated around me, a dark mist that prickled and burned, but the horrible thoughts of sacrifice didn't overwhelm me.

I joined Tarron, and we walked through the trees, approaching the obelisk. He carried a long silver sword, his posture stiff. Tension tightening my muscles as we neared. The magic grew thicker the closer we got, but our protection held it at bay. Our backup spread out to our left and right, Aeri at my side.

We were only forty feet from the obelisk when the ground cracked open around it. It sounded like thunder booming, and more black smoke billowed up. My skin chilled as figures crawled out of the ground. Their skin was pale white and their hair jet black. Every stitch of clothing on their bodies was the color of midnight, and they bore obsidian blades, the sharpest on earth.

The thorn wolf appeared at my side in that moment, a low growl rumbling through his chest. He pressed his side against my leg, and I felt the prick of his thorns. It was comforting, somehow.

I called on my bow from the ether, heartbeat thundering in my ears. There were a dozen Unseelie Fae. Then two dozen. They moved with a graceful swiftness that was almost eerie, and I began to fire my bow.

My arrows sailed true, piercing one Fae in the chest and another in the eye. They tumbled backward, shrieking. The rest of our troops joined in, firing arrows or magic. No one dared use fire in the King's Grove—the trees were far too valuable.

That didn't stop the Unseelie Fae, however. They lit the place up, and two of our troops dedicated themselves to shooting blasts of water at every flaming tree.

I fired arrows as quickly as I could, taking out Fae after Fae. But they kept coming, climbing out of the ground like huge, evil insects.

Tarron and I had gained almost no ground. We needed

to reach the crevasses from which the Unseelie crawled, but it took all we had to stay alive and avoid their deadly attacks.

Next to me, Tarron shot blasts of light from his palms. It was so bright it blinded me to look at it, and when the light hit an Unseelie Fae, the creature shrieked and tumbled backward.

As if he noticed me watching, he grunted in answer. "Sunlight."

Genius. The trees would like it. The Unseelie Fae would not.

All of the Fae used some kind of earth magic. At times, the roots beneath my feet would reach up to grab my legs. I had to abandon my bow in favor of a blade to slice them away. They twisted tightly, trying to drag me down. I hacked at them, cutting them away.

My sister fought the same battle, hacking at the roots. They fell away from her, useless, and she continued to slice at oncoming Fae with her blade.

The Fae on our side manipulated the tree limbs, using magic to twist them downward. The limbs grabbed the Unseelie and hoisted them into the hair, squeezing them until they died. Screams echoed from above, and some of the Unseelie managed to use their own magic to wither the tree limbs until they were dropped to the ground.

The thorn wolf was fast, lunging for the Unseelie who fell out of the trees and tearing at their flesh with his fangs. When an enemy would get too close to the wolf, he'd shoot huge wooden spikes from his fur, never missing. The Fae would fall back, screaming.

Breaths heaving, I dodged a fireball that nearly took off my head, and noticed Aeri doing the same. A second fireball glanced against my arm, making pain flare. Panic surged on its heels. There were so many of them.

The Fae were nearly upon us now, four of them headed right toward Aeri and me. Two others joined them.

I caught Aeri's eye. "Lightning?"

She nodded sharply, then sliced her palm with her blade. I did the same, calling upon the electric magic within me. This had been one of the first magics we'd made together, one of many desperate attempts to escape captivity as children.

We sprinted apart from each other, making sure we stood on either side of the Unseelie who were running toward us. With the lightning crackling inside my chest, I raised my hand. I forced the magic through my arm and out through the bloody cut. Aeri did the same, and our lightning met in the middle, forming a glinting rope of electricity that we dragged across the oncoming Fae.

It sliced through them, lighting them up like fireworks. Aeri and I ran forward, managing to take out eight of the bastards. When we got too close to a cluster of trees, we killed the magic.

I grinned at her, darkly satisfied. It'd been iffy to try lightning in the King's Grove, but there was now a pathway to the crevasse that led to the Unseelie realm.

"Tarron!" I shouted.

He caught sight of me, then the pathway, and sprinted for me. Two Unseelie lunged for him, but he took off their heads with impossibly fast blows of his sword.

I ran for the crevasse that cut deep into the earth, leaves crunching underfoot. A root reached up to grab me, but I jumped over it and kept going. I could hear Tarron running from behind. As I neared the deep pit that opened up right in front of the obelisk, the dark magic that billowed out grew stronger. Cold began to seep into my chest, the protection charm starting to falter.

I fought it and the natural darkness within me, focusing on my task and all the lives that I could save. Tarron appeared at my side, and a moment later, we reached the crevasse. It shimmered with dark light at my feet.

A portal.

He grabbed my hand, and together, we jumped.

The ether swallowed me, spinning me around through space until my stomach lurched. It spit me out in the darkness of an underground world. I gripped Tarron's hand tightly as I stumbled, barely managing to keep my footing. Magic sparked within me, strange and foreign. This whole place felt weird.

Familiar?

It pulsed inside me, magic flaring to life. Almost like recognition.

No.

I blinked, trying to adjust my vision.

Instinct made me look up, and I caught sight of an Unseelie Fae about to land on me.

I darted out of the way, dragging Tarron with me. The Unseelie Fae landed in a graceful crouch, then lunged for us, black claws outstretched and obsidian blade glinting. I kicked the sword away, then stabbed him in the stomach with my own blade. As I twisted, Tarron turned to fight another two Fae. They'd been waiting for us—guards, perhaps.

I finished off the Fae who was stuck on my blade, while Tarron blasted the other two with pure sunlight.

When all three had fallen, I stood tense, panting, every sense alert for another attack.

Tarron looked ready to pounce, every inch of him screaming with violence. His horns had come out, along with his black eyes and fangs. He even had massive wings sprouted from his back. They looked like silver lightning, ephemeral yet powerful.

"We need to hurry," he said. "We've taken out the advance guard, but eventually, they'll send more."

I nodded, finally taking in our surroundings. The first thing I did was check on my transport power. Relief flowed through me when I didn't feel any kind of powerful blocking spell. I could get myself out of here when this was all over.

I looked at Tarron. "Can you transport?"

"I can."

"Good." We'd have a way to run for it after detonating the bomb.

I inspected the huge room. We stood inside an enormous underground dome. It was much taller than it was wide, with a broad ledge spiraling around the edges down to the bottom. We were near the top, with a long way to go to get the ground below.

The obelisk speared down from the middle of the domed ceiling, all the way to the floor below. It glowed with faint light, illuminating the entire huge space. Crackling magic—a bit like lightning—shot from it, filling up the entire dome. It terminated when it reached the spiral walkway that led to the bottom, but it would be impossible for Tarron to fly down through the huge open space in the middle. He'd be struck by the lightning as soon as he took flight.

"We need to blow it up from the bottom," Tarron said. "It's the only way to destroy it."

I nodded, then started down the long ramp that hugged the walls of the massive cavern. We ran as fast as we could, spiraling into the depths. We moved so fast that when the floor in front of us broke away, it took the ground right out from under my feet.

A scream burst from my throat as I plummeted, then a rush of air picked me up. It tore at my hair as it carried me back up toward the spot from which I'd fallen. Soon, I was level with Tarron, whose wings kept him aloft. He waved his hand, and the wind carried me to stable ground. Only part of the ground had broken away, and I staggered when my feet hit solid rock.

"Oh fates, thank you."

He nodded, and I kept running. I wanted to go more slowly—to watch out for the earth falling away from below me—but we didn't have that kind of time. To be safe, I'd have to mince along, and it just wasn't an option. Not with the Unseelie Fae headed our way, ready to defend their turf.

Anyway, there was always Tarron, who could control the wind.

I'd just have to have faith in him.

I kept going, sprinting until my lungs wanted to burst.

We were halfway down when we passed by a huge hole in the wall that acted as an entrance. Four Unseelie lunged out, their obsidian blades drawn. Each was tall and slender, with burning dark eyes and sleek black hair. One of them lunged right for me, and I darted left, spinning back to face him as I raised my blade.

He was fast, though, and managed to grab my arm. I winced and yanked it free.

His widened eyes met mine. Recognition flared. "You."

"What? Do you know me?"

He swung his blade for me, and I darted back, sucking in my stomach to avoid a nasty evisceration.

"Do you know my mother?" I hissed, making sure that Tarron couldn't hear. I pointed to the obelisk. "Is this her magic?"

The Fae lunged for me again, swiping his sword toward me. He nicked my side, and pain flared. I darted back, determined not to kill him before I had my answers.

Light flashed from behind him, and he blasted

forward, falling to his face, a massive blackened hole in his back.

Tarron.

He'd saved me.

Damn it.

He was taking out two more of the Unseelie Fae with sunlight that made them hiss and shriek.

Another Fae appeared to my left. She showed no sign of recognizing me, so I lunged for her, and our blades slammed together. Though hers was made of obsidian—which should have been brittle since it was made of volcanic glass—it didn't shatter. The power of the blow radiated up my arm. I yanked my blade back and tried again, slicing at her arm.

Her sword slashed at my leg, making agony surge. I gasped, trying to ignore it. I managed to dart out of the way before she could cause too much damage, then I landed a blow to her gut. Her dark eyes widened, and she hissed at me.

I kicked her in the stomach, dislodging her from my blade. She teetered toward the edge of the walkway, her arms whirling. Then she fell. I leaned over the edge to watch black wings sprout from her back, but they didn't help. The electricity shooting from the crystal obelisk in the middle of the room crackled into her, making it impossible for her to fly. She slammed to the ground.

I pulled back, not wanting to look anymore.

"Let's go." Tarron led the way, sprinting deeper into the cavern.

We were nearly to the bottom when a smoke wolf appeared. Far larger than a normal wolf, the creature had a body made of ephemeral black smoke and pearly white fangs. They dripped with a ruby red venom, and its eyes blazed a bright neon green.

A growl sounded from my left.

I looked over.

The thorn wolf.

"Your friend is here to protect you," Tarron said.

I looked at the one-eyed thorn wolf. "You sure you can take him?"

My wolf just growled louder, crouching low in an attack position. Despite the fact that he had only one eye and a very ragged ear, he looked tough. He probably looked tough *because* of those things. Like he'd lost the eye in a battle that had prepared him for this very moment.

He lunged for the smoke wolf, which turned to flesh and blood when the two collided. Jaws snapped and claws raked.

"Come on." Tarron grabbed my arm, and we ran around the side of the two fighting wolves.

I spared the thorn wolf one last worried glance, then kept going. He'd chosen to come here. He must have known he was up to the task.

We sprinted the rest of the way down without running into anyone. As soon as we reached the bottom, shouts sounded from high above. I looked up, catching sight of some Unseelie Fae who'd appeared at the very top of the spiral ramp. They pointed to us, then ran.

"We only have a few minutes," Tarron said. "They won't be slowed by the protections like we were."

I nodded, hurrying forward.

We stood on the broad flat bottom of the cavern. In the distance, right in the middle of the room, the crystal obelisk speared into the ground.

Between us and the obelisk lay an enormous coiled snake. The huge beast had its body pressed against the wall, blocking us from approaching the obelisk. If we wanted to get over, we'd have to climb. There was no way to fly—the electric currents that shot from the obelisk filled the air down here as well.

"He'll wake if we step on him," Tarron whispered.

I nodded, my gaze going toward the huge head that slumbered nearby. The eyes were closed and the powerful body relaxed, but it wouldn't stay that way for long.

"We need to contain it," I said.

Tarron frowned, clearly thinking. "I can bind it in tree roots. There are some in this earth—I can sense them. But he'll wake before I'm done."

"I'll try to keep him asleep."

"You need to do better than try."

"I'll manage." I pointed at him. "Now get ready. No dawdling. I won't have long."

He nodded, then approached the dirt wall that was closest. I crept closer to the snake's head, marveling at how thick its body was. I'd seen bigger snakes before—mind-bogglingly enormous ones—but I'd never been so close to one. His body was thicker around than I was tall, and his head was the size of a bus. Air whooshed from his nose as he slept, and I moved aside so it didn't blow on me. Snake breath was not my favorite.

Quickly, I sliced my forefinger and called upon my magic. I'd seen Aeri do this spell before, and hoped I could make it work just as well.

I envisioned the power of sleep, of controlling someone else's mind so they didn't wake. I pressed my hand to the snake's neck and fed my magic into him.

"Sleep," I whispered. "Stay asleep."

The snake shuddered, and carefully, I fed it more of my magic. It was a combination of suggestion and sleep magic, and it worked.

I chanced a glance at Tarron, who had pressed his hands against the dirt wall nearest us. His magic swelled on the air, bringing with it the scent of the forest and the feel of a breeze.

Up above, the Unseelie Fae ran down the spiral walkway, getting ever closer. More of them had appeared, and I had a feeling they weren't the last we'd see.

15

As if he'd heard me, Tarron's magic flared more strongly. His aura shined a bright green, and the taste of honey was thick on my tongue.

All around, roots began to burst free of the earth. They reached for the snake, coiling around him, twisting around the cylindrical body and binding it tight to the cavern wall.

The snake shifted, clearly irritated, and I tried to increase the strength of my sleep magic. It didn't work.

I'd need more blood. This was hardly enough for a snake of this size.

The creature's eyes burst open, yellow and bright. They pinned me with a laser stare, and the mouth gaped, fangs sharp. The creature hissed loudly, and I flinched.

"That's enough," Tarron said. "We need to hurry."

Anxiety shivered through me, but I let go of the snake, letting the sleep magic fade away. The snake struggled and thrashed, but the root bindings held firm.

Tarron climbed over the snake's back first, staying low to avoid the crackling electric shafts that shot from the obelisk. As long as we stayed really low, we were safe from them.

I followed, keeping my belly pressed to the snake's back as I climbed over. On the other side, we ran toward the obelisk in a crouch. Tarron removed the bomb from his pack and placed it at the base of the obelisk. I added the little amplifying charm that I'd made, but most of the power would come from me.

I touched the glowing red bomb one last time to get a feel for its magic, then looked at Tarron. "Ready?"

"Ready."

We ran back to the snake, which was still bound. We'd work from back here in hopes of avoiding the blast. As long as the snake stayed contained, it should work.

I checked on the Unseelie Fae one last time. They were almost to us, running down the ramp. There was no more time for me to hunt for answers about my past. This was it. We had to destroy this thing and go.

"Go!" I said, calling upon my amplification magic.

I let it fill me, imagining the bomb exploding in glorious fashion. I'd make it bigger and stronger than it could be otherwise. As Tarron called upon his sunlight magic—our fuse—I recalled what the bomb had felt like. The massive combustive magic that had sparked within it.

Tarron threw his hands out and shot a blast of sunlight right at the bomb. It ignited, exploding toward the ceiling.

I used my magic to amplify it, sending the blast upward through the base of the obelisk.

The crystal cracked from within, the magic fighting that of the blast. Heat from the explosion billowed toward us, and Tarron used his wind magic to blast it back. Great gusts of air burst from his hands, driving the flame back toward the obelisk.

Still, it heated my face, and I squinted against the bright red light. I strained to keep my magic going, forcing the bomb's explosion to grow as I amplified its power.

The Unseelie Fae neared us, their shouts of rage washing over me. I used it to fuel my work. Those bastards had caused the deaths of hundreds. I didn't want to think about the fact that one of them had thought I was familiar.

It all but confirmed my mother was one of them.

My heartbeat thundered in my ears. The obelisk cracked all the way up to the top, the bottom already shattered from the force of the explosion. More of the crystal fell away as the entire thing broke apart.

The Unseelie were only yards away now. Tarron's magic was faltering. So was mine. Exhaustion dragged at me, nearly taking me to my knees. I was almost tapped out.

"Come on!" Taron grabbed my arm. "Let's get out of here."

I didn't need telling twice. I killed the amplification magic and called upon my transport powers. They stuttered at first, exhaustion making me slow. The Unseelie were almost to me, so close that I could see their white fangs.

Then the ether sucked me up, spinning me through space. I imagined the King's Grove, sending myself back to the battle so I could check on Aeri.

We arrived in a wasteland. Half of the trees were burnt to a crisp, and there were Unseelie bodies everywhere. A few Seelie as well, their red cloaks sprawled on the forest floor.

The obelisk that had stood in the middle of the grove was nothing but ash.

Thank fates.

I spun from it, searching for Aeri. I spotted her kneeling next to a fallen Seelie, making sure he was okay. Fortunately, it looked like he was.

I ran to her and dropped to my knees. "Are you all right?"

"Yeah." Her gaze flicked over me. "You?"

"Yes. Fine." I searched the grove. "Any casualties?"

"Three. I don't know who, but that's what Luna said."

"Damn." My heart hurt for those who'd died here today. I turned, searching for Tarron.

He knelt by the body of another fallen Seelie, his brow set and his mouth a grim line.

What should I do? The job was done. The obelisk destroyed. The black magic that had filled this place was gone. I had his sworn blood oath that he wouldn't reveal what I was.

It was time to leave.

I reached for Aeri. "Come on. Let's go."

We needed to get out of here. I hadn't found my

mother today, but that place had felt almost familiar. And one of the Unseelie Fae had recognized me.

That was too much to be a coincidence. It made my insides chill and my heart race. I had to get out of here.

Three nights later, after a lot of thinking and general misery, I met Aeri at Potions & Pastilles, our favorite coffee shop/bar. It was located on the other side of town, on Factory Row, where most of the antique stores did their business. This entire part of town was refurbished factory buildings from the eighteenth century, with huge glass windows and lots of exposed brick.

A very different feel from Darklane, which was older, but I'd grown to like it over the years, at least a little bit. As usual, I wore my Blood Sorceress Mordaca attire—hair, makeup, dress. If I was in Magic's Bend, I was most comfortable dressed like this.

I hadn't seen Tarron since I'd left, nor heard from him. I expected to, though. We'd shared two mind-blowing kisses and some devastating personal stuff. Not to mention the fact that I was his *Mograh*. He was going to try to ignore it, but could he?

Except, I might be Unseelie Fae, a secret that I needed to keep from him forever.

Maybe it would be better if he never came.

Potions & Pastilles was quiet when I entered, since it

was midafternoon. After the coffee rush and before it turned into a whiskey bar for the evening. Local art hung on the walls, and mason-jar lamps dangled from the ceiling.

Connor looked up from behind the bar, his floppy dark hair speckled with flour. As usual, he wore a band T-shirt. Jim Croce today.

"Hey, Mordaca." He waved a flour-covered hand. "What will it be?"

"Double espresso, but no rush."

He nodded and got to work with the shiny espresso machine, and I took a seat near the window in the corner, as far from the coffee bar as possible. I had some things to say, and I didn't really want them overheard.

I tapped my foot and stuck a butterscotch hard candy in my mouth, barely managing to resist crunching down on it.

Magic sparked on the air next to me, and I looked down.

The thorn wolf had appeared. He was the size of a huge dog, but he looked even bigger, squished between the tables. His thorny coat looked out of place in the coffee shop, and his one good eye was glued to my face.

"Hey, buddy."

His tongue lolled out of his mouth in a weird smile.

I petted his head, careful to go with the grain of the thorns, which lay down flat there. They were smooth underhand. Quite nice, really.

"Got a new friend?" Connor asked.

"Apparently so. Can he stay?"

"Sure. What'll he have?"

"Do you have any bacon?"

Burn's ears perked up.

"We sure do. I'll bring it over."

"Thanks."

Aeri arrived a few minutes later, and after putting in her order, joined me.

"Hey, new friend?" Aeri asked.

"Yeah. Burnthistle. Burn for short."

She petted him carefully, leaning down to say, "My hellcat Wally will love you."

"How's Declan?"

"Good. Now that he knows who stole that bomb—and that it's been deployed—he can take a few days off."

"Ah, right. That was convenient." He'd been hunting the thief who'd stolen the bomb Tarron had deployed.

So, technically, he'd been hunting Tarron. He'd just never found him. And never would, since the Fae king so rarely left his realm.

"Hey, how are you?" She leaned forward, eyes keen. "I haven't seen you in two days. You've been like a ghost."

"Been doing some thinking."

"About Tarron?"

"Him, yeah. But mostly something else."

"What else?"

Connor delivered our drinks, and we thanked him. Burn gobbled down the bacon so fast I barely saw it.

Connor saluted. "Just let me know if you need anything else."

I waited until he was out of earshot before I leaned toward Acri. Nerves made my skin prickle. "I've been keeping a secret from you."

Her brows shot up. "What?"

"A big one. Kind of."

"Like, how big?"

"It's something that's big but doesn't really matter, but I've been keeping it to myself for years because I'm a weirdo." The words came out in a rush.

"Okay, now you're freaking me out."

"We're only half-sisters."

"We're...what?"

"Different moms. Aunt told me, not you."

"But why? I don't understand." Her brow creased. The coffee sat forgotten in front of her.

She didn't seem mad, but yeah, she seemed very confused.

"She used it as a tool to control me. She knew that you were the only good thing I had, and she thought that if she told you that I was half evil, you'd leave me. Or, at least, she made me believe that."

"That's bullshit."

"I know that now. I've known it for years." Yeah, it'd taken some time to believe it, but I *did* know it. "But back then, when I was scared and hungry and cold all the time, I believed her."

"And you always were stronger, so of course she'd want

to control you. To get you to make more magic."

"You always thought I did it to protect you. But in reality, I did it to protect myself from you knowing what I was."

"Of course you did it to protect me. You were just surviving. If you hadn't, I never would have. We needed each other. We still do." She reached across the table and gripped my hands. "Oh, Mari."

I squeezed hers back. I might not like touching, but the rule didn't extend to Aeri.

"Why didn't you tell me sooner?"

I shrugged. "I didn't want to think about it. At first, it was because I believed Aunt's lies. Then, once we'd escaped and I stopped believing, I didn't want to think about it at all. I didn't want it to be true, and if I never thought about it, it wasn't."

"Yeah, because if you thought about it, you'd have to deal with it."

"Exactly."

"Will you look for the other half of your family?"

"That's the thing. I have been." I told her about the magical signature that accompanied the crystal obelisk and how it was similar to my mother's. And about the Unseelie Fae who had recognized me. "I think it triggered something inside me. I've felt different since going there. Like maybe a change is happening."

"You don't know if you are half Unseelie Fae. Not for sure. And even if you are, you are who you choose to be, Mari. It doesn't have to make a difference."

"I hope you're right." And she was right. It wasn't one

hundred percent certain that I was Unseelie Fae. And it didn't make me a different person. I was the same Mari I'd always been.

Aeri leaned forward and gripped my hand. "You were right about one thing though. It doesn't make any difference to me."

I smiled at her, glad that I'd finally said something.

Later that night, I lingered at the edge of the dance floor at UnderRealm, the hottest club in town. The Council of Demon Slayers wanted me to deal with a Korcha demon that had been lurking around the premises lately. They liked to steal souls, and this was the perfect place to do it. Crowded, dark, everyone was distracted.

The job should be a one-and-done deal—they weren't great fighters when they were alone—but it seemed that the demon wasn't going to show. It was already after one in the morning, and there was no sign of him.

I leaned against the wall near the back and scanned the dance floor. My back prickled, almost as if the magic inside me was congregating there. It'd been doing that for the last three days, and it was weird. I shifted, trying to make the feeling stop. It was probably just residual achiness from the battle.

The bass in the music thumped through the room, making the wall shake against my back. Supernaturals danced in the middle of the club, most of them dressed in black. I was in my fight wear, but with the zipper pulled down to show my usual cleavage and my makeup, I fit right in.

I popped a grandma candy in my mouth and sucked on the butterscotch, wishing for a perfectly chilled Manhattan and a long nap.

"Mari. Mordaca." Tarron's voice came from the left, carrying easily over the music.

I stiffened, swallowing the candy.

Holy fates.

I turned to see if I'd been imagining things.

Nope.

Tarron stood against the wall to my left, only five feet away. He wore an impeccable slim-cut navy suit, and though it was human attire, he looked so perfect and deadly in it that he appeared entirely out of place here on earth. His dark hair shined beneath the pulsing club lights, and his green eyes never strayed from my face.

Still impossibly handsome, of course. Still a little scary.

Too bad I liked scary.

Tension tightened the air between us. He moved closer until he stood in front of me.

I tilted my head up to meet his gaze. My fight wear didn't include my usual heels, of course, and the flat-soled black boots made me shorter than I liked. "Tarron. What are you doing here?"

"You disappeared after the battle. Why?"

"Job was done."

"And you just ran off?"

"You wanted to see me?"

"Yes." The words seemed dragged from him. "I wanted to ignore what's between us, but I can't."

I raised a brow. "It's just fate and some old Fae thing. I'm not going to let it determine my life."

"It's more than fate." The expression on his face was so intense I shivered. "You're smart, strong, stubborn, beautiful. It's *you* that draws me, not some ancient magical decree."

A small smile tugged at my lips. I was secretly pleased by his words, though also seriously nervous, given what I suspected of my heritage. I'd wanted to see him, too, though. Even though I shouldn't.

"So, you really don't want to ignore what's between us?" I asked, unable to stop myself.

"I can't." The words seemed almost torn from him. "I owe a debt to my people, but I want this too. I want you."

My breath caught. *I want you.*

I wanted him too.

I wanted him so badly it was like a hunger eating me alive. There was just something about him. About our connection. There could be something between us.

Something real.

Tension thrummed in the air between us. Until now, every interaction of ours had been fraught with suspicion and attraction.

This was no different.

But his confession...

That made it different.

His forest scent wrapped around me, an almost literal breath of fresh air in the hot club. His nearness made my head spin as I remembered our kiss. I watched him, almost vibrating with desire.

I couldn't resist.

I moved toward him, and his mouth crashed down on mine, warm and skilled.

I moaned as his lips moved, drawing me into a haze of passion. Heat surged through me as he gripped my waist and pulled me to him. I pressed myself against his hard chest, reveling in his strength. When I sank my hands into his hair, he groaned low in his throat.

Images of us together flashed in my mind. Of all the things we could do.

I breathed in his scent. Every inch of him blazed like fire, and I couldn't get enough. He pressed me back against the wall and I moaned. All around us, the club pulsed with music.

Heat rose inside me, magic as well. It flared to life in my chest, as if touching him lit up something deep in my soul. I was like a match, and he was gasoline.

Magic sparked through my veins, rising up from deep within me.

Unseelie Fae.

The words flashed in my mind. The suspicion.

Energy rose within me. Tarron's kiss made my breath come short and my head spin, but I couldn't ignore what was going on inside me. It was a mix of desire and something else. Something different.

Like a change.

I pulled back, the energy too much for me to contain. I met Tarron's gaze. He'd shifted, his horns curving around the back of his head and his eyes black.

I gasped as the magic surged within me, seeming to congregate around my back. It exploded out of me, and I stumbled. Confusion welled. Magic clouded my mind.

Tarron's eyes flicked upward, his gaze going to a spot just over my left shoulder. I looked back, spotting an ephemeral flicker of light.

Wings.

I had wings made of light.

Holy fates, what was happening?

Was this the strange energy I'd been feeling the last few days? Had the magic finally burst to the surface?

That was the only explanation. This transition that had started a while ago, probably as far back as my entry into the Unseelie realm. I'd felt it then, almost a familiarity. But I'd ignored it. Kissing Tarron had somehow been the push it needed. He was one of my strongest connections to the Fae world, and it had sparked something within me.

Horror spread through me, but something else as well. A spark of magic. The darkness inside me, unfurling.

I could feel it.

I was Unseelie Fae.

One of the evil Fae.

The ones who had poisoned his realm, killed his people. Resulted in the death of his brother by his own hand.

I turned back to him, catching sight of the horror on his face.

Oh shit.

He knew.

THANK YOU FOR READING!

I hope you enjoyed reading this book as much as I enjoyed writing it. Reviews are *so* helpful to authors. I really appreciate all reviews, both positive and negative. If you want to leave one, you can do so on Amazon or GoodReads.

AUTHOR'S NOTE

Thank you for reading *Trial by Fae!* If you've read any of my other books, you might know that I like to include historical places and mythological elements. I always discuss them in the author's note. In fact, you're probably thinking "another one of these things?" Yep!

Many of the locations in this book were inspired by a recent trip to Scotland to visit an old friend. We're both archaeologists and our idea of a good time is wandering around the countryside in search of old stuff. Sure, there are some fancier words for what we look for, but that's what it really boils down to. Looking at something ancient and trying to figure out what people once did with it.

Kilmartin Glen in western Scotland is home to hundreds of ancient stone monuments, so that's where we headed for this trip. And it was perfect, considering that I wanted Mordaca's story to have a Fae angle. While there are many different types of Fae according to the local lore in different countries, the Seelie and Unseelie Fae were perfect for this book as they are the Scottish version.

Most of places in the book were based upon real historical monuments. In one of her first challenges, Burnthistle led Mari to a flat stone covered with carvings pecked into the stone. They are based upon the Achnabreck Rock Art, and look roughly like spirals. They are actually central cup marks surrounded by concentric circles and they were created more than 4,500 years ago. Archaeologist and scholars speculate about their purpose, but no one really knows. There are hundreds of them all over Kilmartin, however, and they're really quite amazing. They even decorate some of the standing stones, and scholars think it's possible that later people may have used older decorated stones (that once laid flat on the ground) and set them upright for a new purpose.

The chambered cairn that Mari visits is based upon one in Kilmartin Glen called Nether Largie South. A chambered cairn is essentially a pile of rocks with a passageway in the middle that humans can enter. They were often used as burial sites. Sometimes the people were buried as bodies and other times they were cremated and put into clay jars called beakers. In the case of Nether Largie South, there were three beakers containing burial remains and flint arrowheads, which would have likely been a status item or symbolic in some way. Mari saw these but just stepped around them, as it would be really uncool to mess with them. The chambered cairn at Nether Largie South was initially built between 5,600 to 5,500 years ago, which makes it far older than the rock art I mention above. It was reused for later burials around 4,300 years ago, which was when the beaker pots were added. It was remodeled once again a few generations later, when it adopted the form that we see today.

The stone circle that Mari enters is inspired by the standing stones in Kilmartin, though there isn't a circle quite that large in the Glen. There are standing stones arranged in lines but no circles quite that big.

The large hill that Mari climbs to get a better view is based upon a hill fort in Kilmartin called Dunadd Fort. Today, it is little more than broken walls and a well—which Mari notices as she walks—but it is still spectacular and provides an amazing view of the glen and the sea beyond. 1,300 hundred years ago, it was originally the heart of the Gaelic kingdom of Dál Riata. The descendants of the Dál Riata kings became the first kings of Scotland. Their people, known as the *Scotti*, would one day become the first Scots.

The Wish Stone is based upon a carved stone ball found at the base of Dunadd fort. Local legend says that these stone balls have magical powers and were abandoned by fairies in a farmhouse at the base of the hill fort. This stone ball is not the only one of its kind—four thousand years ago, these carved balls were made all across Scotland, with a larger concentration in the North-East.

I think that's it for the history and mythology in *Trial by Fae*. I think it was probably my favorite to write, and I hope you enjoyed it and will come back for more Mordaca and Aerdeca.

ACKNOWLEDGMENTS

Thank you, Ben, for everything. There would be no books without you.

Thank you to Jena O'Connor and Lindsey Loucks for your excellent editing. The book is immensely better because of you! Thank you Eleonora, Richard, and Aisha for you helpful comments about typos.

Thank you to Orina Kafe for the beautiful cover art.

ABOUT LINSEY

Before becoming a writer, Linsey Hall was a nautical archaeologist who studied shipwrecks from Hawaii and the Yukon to the UK and the Mediterranean. She credits fantasy and historical romances with her love of history and her career as an archaeologist. After a decade of tromping around the globe in search of old bits of stuff that people left lying about, she settled down and started penning her own romance novels. Her Dragon's Gift series draws upon her love of history and the paranormal elements that she can't help but include.

COPYRIGHT